DISNEP
PIRATES of the CARIBBEAN
LEGENDS OF THE BRETHREN COURT

Wild Waters

Rob Kidd

Based on the earlier adventures of characters created
for the theatrical motion picture,
"Pirates of the Caribbean: The Curse of the Black Pearl"
Screen Story by Ted Elliott & Terry Rossio and
Stuart Beattie and Jay Wolpert,
Screenplay by Ted Elliott & Terry Rossio,
And characters created for the theatrical motion pictures
"Pirates of the Caribbean: Dead Man's Chest" and
"Pirates of the Caribbean: At World's End"
written by Ted Elliott & Terry Rossio

DISNEP PRESS

New York

PIRATES of the CARIBBEAN

LEGENDS OF THE BRETHREN COURT

Wild Waters

PROLOGUE

Barbara Huntington had a fierce headache.

Spying on pirates was much more annoying than she'd expected. Barbara had thought she was being very clever when she gave her unwitting accomplice, Marcella Magliore, a supernatural hand mirror. That way Barbara could see and hear everything Marcella did—and, by extension, everything that was happening on the *Black Pearl*.

The good news was that it had worked so far.

The Huntingtons knew exactly where the Pirate Lord Jack Sparrow was going next: Africa. He was looking for the Pirate Lord of the Atlantic Ocean. That much they had overheard through the powerful mirror, although they weren't exactly sure *why* Sparrow was looking for him.

But the bad news was that in order to spy on the *Pearl*, Barbara and Benedict had to spy on Marcella. And as they had quickly discovered, Marcella *loved* looking at herself in the mirror. And talking to herself (or rather, whining to herself) in the mirror. And checking her teeth in the mirror, and plucking her eyebrows in the mirror, and using the mirror to peer up her nose, and all kinds of other horrible things that Barbara could happily have lived without seeing.

Barbara flung the mirror down on the floor of her husband's cabin and rubbed her forehead. Her dazzling red hair was piled high in a crown of curls around her pale face, and she wore one of the bright blue silk gowns Benedict had purchased for her when they fled to Delhi after the humiliating battle at Sri Sumbhajee's palace. They hadn't had time for the gown to be fitted properly, so she wasn't entirely pleased with it, but Benedict assured her that it was effective nonetheless.

She was lying on thick white- and gold-colored furs, which were draped over the couch in Benedict's austerely decorated cabin. Normally she did not spend time on his ship, preferring the luxuries of their home in Hong Kong, so he had arranged the cabin according to his own bleak, unadorned preferences. There were none of the little comforts she liked: few pillows, hardly any mirrors, and no curtains at all. The sun beat painfully through the tiny windows, shining right in her eyes.

The *Peacock* rocked and swayed, making her headache worse. They hadn't seen land in days, and the last time they had stopped, she hadn't even had time to buy herself a new pair of shoes. Benedict was driving his crew like a man possessed.

Hearing the mirror clatter on the smooth wooden floorboards, Benedict looked up from the charts on his desk and smirked. "Not going well?"

"That girl is horrendous," said Barbara with an aggrieved sigh. "She's worse than those irritating monkeys I had killed after they stole my breakfast that one morning, remember? If I have to hear about 'dear, handsome Diego' and his furious Spanish princess one more time, I'm going to throw someone overboard. Start thinking about who you can spare."

Captain Huntington snorted. "All of them. This useless crew can't even catch up to a bunch of half-wit pirates. I should keelhaul the lot of them."

"It's not really their fault," Barbara said, draping a turquoise silk scarf over her eyes. "You heard the pirates in the mirror. They say the *Black Pearl* is the fastest ship in the entire ocean."

"Yes." Benedict's eyes gleamed. "What an excellent prize it will make. A reward for all the trouble I've gone to."

He picked up a letter emblazoned with the seal of the East India Trading Company from his desk, and crumpled it in his pale, bony hand. "The nerve of the Company—telling me to return to my post! This mission is far more important than anything I had to do in Hong Kong."

"Don't worry about them," Barbara said. "Focus on capturing Jack Sparrow. He must pay for what happened in Hong Kong. And again in India."*

Benedict Huntington was always pale, but the thought of the indignities he'd suffered

*See Legends of the Brethren Court Vols. 2 and 3

lately made his skeletal face even paler with fury. Several Pirate Lords had been within his grasp— first Sao Feng and Mistress Ching, and then Sri Sumbhajee—but they had all slipped away, all of them escaping to freedom and further pillaging. All because of Jack Sparrow. Oh, Jack would pay dearly. Indeed he would.

He slid another letter toward himself, one that he and Barbara had been studying since leaving India. Evidently another party was as interested in stopping Jack Sparrow as they were. Benedict didn't even know how the letter had appeared on his desk, but he didn't question it. His enemy's enemy was certainly welcome to do as much violence as he liked.

The only thing Benedict didn't know was how to contact this Shadow Lord, or who he was. Or why he hated Jack Sparrow so much. All right, to tell the truth, there were a lot of things he didn't know—like why the Shadow

Lord was using the stationery of the Spanish Pirate Lord, Villanueva. Or why he wanted Benedict to do everything in his power to stop Jack from coming face-to-face with the next Pirate Lord.

But at least Benedict knew something Jack didn't know about this Pirate Lord of the Atlantic Ocean Jack was searching for. From the conversations they'd eavesdropped on—at least, from what they could hear around Marcella's injured sighs and muttered comments—it was clear that Jack didn't even know the current Pirate Lord's name.

Benedict, on the other hand, had a large file sitting in front of him, all about this "King Samuel." And from what he'd learned, he had a feeling the *Peacock* would get a warmer welcome than the *Black Pearl* would. Which was something he could, and definitely *would*, use to his advantage.

A shrill voice came from the mirror on the floor. "Salt pork *again* today? It's horrible stuff! I hate it! Just look what it does to my skin! Am I getting yellower? I think I am! Jean, pay attention to me! Look at my face! Yellower! I'm sure of it!"

Benedict glanced at Barbara, but she refused to move her eyes from behind her scarf. Reluctantly, Benedict picked up the mirror and looked into it. He shuddered at the close-up of Marcella's sharp chin on the other side. She was peering at her skin intently, unaware of her observers. Behind her, Benedict could see the other girl pirate on the *Pearl* practicing her sword-fighting skills with a redheaded pirate. They danced and parried back and forth while Marcella grumbled about how Jean never listened to her, and how it wasn't fair that "poor Diego" always had to be up in the crow's nest, and how swords were stupid anyway.

Then Benedict spotted Jack Sparrow flouncing cheerfully around the deck. He gritted his teeth, wishing he were standing there with his rapier. He'd carve that cheeky smile right off the pirate's face.

A wet splash hit the mirror on Marcella's side, blurring the image. Benedict saw Marcella's fuzzy outline lift her head to the sky.

"Oh, *nooooooooo*," she wailed. "It's *raaaaaiiiiining*! Ew, I'm going to get all wet! Ew, it's going to mess up my hair! I'm going to my hammock, and I'm not coming back until it stops!"

"Promise?" said a pirate's voice in the background.

"I really hate pirates," Marcella snarled at the mirror and then snapped it shut. The image went dark, and now all Benedict could see in the smooth surface was his own pinched face.

At least he could agree with Marcella on one thing. He really, really hated pirates, too.

CHAPTER ONE

Rain splattered down on the deck of the *Black Pearl*, relentlessly drenching the slippery boards and drooping black sails. Pirates huddled under oilcloths or belowdecks, wet and miserable. Gloomy gray clouds filled the sky to every horizon, with even darker clouds visible up ahead.

A lone figure stood at the prow of the *Pearl*, staring out at the endless gray sea. He had been standing there for several hours without moving. His ragged clothes were soaked through, and his hair was plastered to his blank face.

"Oi!" a voice called through the rain.

The figure did not turn around.

Jack Sparrow, captain of the *Black Pearl*, Pirate Lord of the Caribbean, was a busy fellow. He had important things to do. He needed to chart the ship's course to Africa and figure out how to liberate a vial of Shadow Gold from a Pirate Lord he knew nothing about, and he had to do it all before his mysterious illness returned to torment him with nightmares of the angry Shadow Lord. He'd had one particularly awful nightmare in India which he was *fairly* certain had been an actual visit from the Shadow Lord. If so, that meant the evil pirate knew exactly what Jack was up to, which was a bad, bad thing.

If the Shadow Lord got to the vials of Shadow

Gold before Jack did . . . well, all manner of trickery and thievery and sneakery might be required, and really, given the choice, Jack would much prefer *not* confronting the sinister Shadow Lord and *not* being eaten by nasty shadows, thank you very much.

But it was difficult to focus on charts and maps when he was distracted. He leaned a little further out the door of his cabin and squinted through the curtain of steady rain at the man on the foredeck.

"What is he doing out there?"

"Nothin' worth our botherin' about," his first mate, Barbossa, growled from inside the cabin. He tapped the maps and charts on Jack's desk meaningfully, irritated at all the interruptions Jack managed to find whenever they had important ship's business to attend to. "Jaaaaaaaack."

"*Captain* Jaaaaaaack," Jack muttered

absentmindedly. "I mean, I'm all for keeping a weather eye on the horizon, but not when there's so much . . . *weather* involved." He paused, thinking. "I'll just go check on him, shall I?" He threw a coat over his head and popped out the door before Barbossa could stop him.

Barbossa grumbled for a minute before realizing that the coat Jack had grabbed to use as an umbrella was, in fact, Barbossa's own fashionable blue peacoat with the silver buttons. With a snarl, Barbossa threw a glass across the cabin to shatter against the opposite wall.

"Soon," he muttered aloud to himself. "I won't have to put up with this much longer. Soon things will be very different around here." The scheming first mate knew he had to wait until the time was right, and at the moment Jack had too many friends among the crew. Jean, Diego, Billy, Carolina . . . Barbossa was sure he could convince any one of them alone, but together . . . it would never work. But one day his time would come. . . .

Outside, Jack slipped and slid across the open deck and up the wooden steps to the foredeck. He lifted Barbossa's coat and peered out from under it at the sagging face that stared so solemnly out to sea.

"Lovely day," said Jack.

"Lovely day, Captain Jack Sparrow," the zombie said agreeably.

Jack raised an eyebrow at him. Alex the zombie had been raised from his grave by the mystic woman Tia Dalma—the same mystic who had stolen the vials of Shadow Gold from the Shadow Lord in the first place.* She had given the vials to Alex to give to the strongest Pirate Lord, but he had rather misunderstood

*In Vol. 1: *The Caribbean*

the message (that's the trouble with partially decayed brains), and instead distributed one vial apiece to several of the strongest Pirate Lords. Jack had not been one of them, a detail which he still found quite insulting.

So really, it was Alex's fault they were on this journey in the first place. Well, his and Tia Dalma's, as she was the one who sent Jack off to retrieve the vials (and warn the Brethren Court about the menace of the Shadow Lord at the same time). Oh, and it was also the Shadow Lord's fault, for giving Jack a terrible shadow-sickness that could only be cured by drinking all the vials.

Really, it was everyone's fault but Jack's. So if you asked him, it wasn't quite fair that he was the one standing in a downpour trying to convince a zombie—a zombie specifically sent to spy on him for Tia Dalma, mind you—to come in out of the storm.

"Not worried about melting, are you?" Jack asked.

"Not worried about melting, Captain Jack Sparrow," Alex said, his gaze still fixed on the horizon.

Jack eyed the zombie's soggy skin with concerned horror. He didn't really relish the idea of making his pirates mop up Alex's melted remains after the storm passed.

"Right," said Jack. "Well. Quite a bit drier down belowdecks, you know. Much less . . . melty down there."

"I am keeping an eye out for the Shadow Lord, Captain Jack Sparrow," Alex intoned.

"Keeping an eye out?" Jack echoed. That rang a bell. "Ah, yes . . . as I told you to, eh?" Now he remembered giving the zombie an order that morning, although, like most of Jack's orders, it had been tossed flippantly over his shoulder as he dashed from one end of the ship to the other.

16

And, like most of Jack's orders, he was quite surprised to find anyone obeying it. But that was the best and the worst thing about zombies. (Well, one of the worst things. Others included the smell and finding bits of toes left behind in the ratlines.)

"Well, then," Jack said. Rain dripped through a buttonhole in Barbossa's coat and landed on Jack's ear. "Excellent work. Brilliant. Just as I wanted. So. Any sign of him?"

"No," said Alex. "But he has always been good at sneaking up on his enemies, Captain Jack Sparrow."

Jack shivered. That was not what he wanted to hear. "How do you know so much about the Shadow Lord, then?" he asked. "Maybe you're wrong. Maybe he's actually very inept and, and . . . loud and not very good at being sneaky at all, savvy?"

"I doubt he has changed much since I wrote

his biography, Captain Jack Sparrow," Alex said blandly. "Apart from the supernatural forces now under his control, I mean. That's a little different."

Jack blinked. Raindrops splashed in his eyes and he blinked some more. "Hang on," he said. "You wrote the Shadow Lord's *biography*? What, like a book?"

"Certainly, Captain Jack Sparrow," said Alex. "I was his barber. I was there for all his underhanded victories and barbarous deeds." He paused, and a glimmer of personality appeared in his dead eyes. "It was a very good book."

"Must admit it's hard to imagine you having a way with words," Jack said, hunching further under Barbossa's coat. "But good to know. Per'aps you can tell us something useful about him, then."

"He was a cruel man, Captain Jack Sparrow,"

Alex said. "I fear he is even crueler now."

"All right, well, that's enough cheering me up for one day," Jack said. "Go on below and get dry. Not even the Shadow Lord would be out attacking ships in this weather."

"Don't count on it," Alex said gloomily.

The zombie sploshed his way to the hatch and vanished below as Jack hurried back to his cabin, huddled under Barbossa's drenched coat. The wind was starting to pick up, turning the steady downpour into a lashing storm. The wet deck rolled and dove beneath his fine leather boots, and he windmilled his arms to stay upright.

Far above him, another crew member watched the captain fling himself at his cabin door and disappear inside. In the crow's nest, Diego pulled his oilcloth over his head and leaned back against the mast. The terrible weather matched his mood exactly. He felt like he deserved every stinging raindrop and soaking gust of wind. And in any case, even being aloft in the middle of a thunderstorm was preferable to being trapped belowdecks with Carolina and Marcella.

Marcella was somehow convinced that she and Diego were a couple now, because she had kissed him back in India, however much against his will. On the other hand, Carolina, who had also kissed Diego in India, and whom he had very happily kissed back, seemed equally convinced that he and Marcella were a couple— no matter how much he tried to convince her that he felt nothing for Marcella. So Carolina was avoiding him as if he smelled as horrible as Alex, while Marcella kept popping up from nowhere to fling her arms around him or make loud admiring comments into her mirror where he could hear her.

He narrowed his eyes, squinting into the

stormy darkness. Where had that mirror come from? She'd been flashing it around nonstop since they left Suvarnadurg. Did someone in India give it to her? Sri Sumbhajee's wife Parvati had given Carolina a moonstone for protection . . . but nobody liked Marcella enough to give her things. And it was an odd silver mirror with a European design; he hadn't seen anything like it in Sumbhajee's palace.

Diego shrugged, sending a pool of water rippling down his back. Ah, well. The mirror was strange, he figured, but it probably wasn't worth thinking about.

Of course, he was quite wrong about that.

CHAPTER TWO

"It's never going to end," Billy groaned as his hammock bounced and swayed furiously under him. His face was green with seasickness, something that hadn't bothered him in years. He closed his eyes, trying to avoid the sight of the jolting, swinging lanterns that lit the stuffy lower deck. "We'll be sailing through this storm for the rest of our lives."

"Well, that won't be long," Jean moaned from his hammock, clutching his stomach woefully.

"Since we're definitely going to shipwreck soon. Or starve. I'm going to die without ever seeing Lakshmi again. I can't keep anything down. And I'm SO HUNGRY."

The storm had been raging for days. There was no way to tell where they were anymore, or even whether it was day or night. The *Black Pearl* shook and groaned as the waves battered it, and empty rum bottles rolled across the floor below the hammocks. It was a sign of how seasick all the pirates were that not a one of them lamented the lack of rum; they were too ill to want anything at all.

"Jack says it might be supernatural," Carolina said. She clung to the door frame, trying to stay upright. She was determined to be the strongest, healthiest sailor of them all . . . but even she couldn't imagine enduring another terrible night of sleepless nausea and howling gale-force winds.

"Don't go spreading that around," Billy said. "Even if it is probably true."

"Who would do this to us?" Jean asked. "Can the Shadow Lord send storms, too?"

"No," said Alex's gloomy voice from the far corner of the room, where he had been banished as far as possible from the hammocks. "He can't do that. Sometimes a storm is just a storm."

"And sometimes it's the end of the world, isn't it?" Billy muttered.

"It *is* the end of the world!" Marcella wailed. "I'm going to die surrounded by horrible, horrible, smelly pirates!" Her hammock and Carolina's were hung behind a makeshift curtain, separating them from the other pirates. Carolina made a determined effort to sleep there only when Marcella was elsewhere, but Marcella had been lying in her hammock and whining for almost the entire length of the storm. None of them could see Jean's cousin in her screened-off area, but they could all most definitely *hear* her. "Oh, *where* is Diego?" Marcella went on. "Why doesn't he come take *care* of me?"

"I'm going back on deck," said Carolina, staggering toward the ladder. "I'd rather die wet than listen to this. Or put up with this smell any longer."

The lower deck, normally not the freshest-smelling place, stank worse than it ever had, with all the pirates crowded together in the dank underbelly of the ship. The tarpaulins lashed across the hatchway kept the rain out, but they also made the space below even darker and stuffier.

Carolina lifted the hatch to climb out, prompting a yell of protest from some of the pirates belowdecks as a gush of water poured down the ladder. She hauled herself onto the deck and slammed the hatch behind her.

The wind immediately tugged her long dark hair loose and sent it flying around her face. She'd lost her hat two days earlier when it went sailing over the rail. Jack had looked horrified when she told him. He'd clutched his own hat to his head and refused to come out of his cabin ever since then, just in case.

The only good thing Carolina could say about the storm was that at least it was warm and tropical. She much preferred that to the freezing rain she remembered from her childhood in Spain. Her bare feet were soaking wet as she splashed through the two inches of water on the deck, but at least they weren't also numb with cold.

She glanced up at the masts looming over her and saw a figure huddled far above in the crow's nest. Diego was up there again, although she was sure he couldn't see anything useful ahead of them in this storm. It was impossible even to navigate; they just had to cross their fingers and hope the storm would deliver them somewhere near Africa. Jack had actually stationed Catastrophe Shane, the worst pirate he'd ever had on his ship, at the wheel, figuring he couldn't do any more damage than the storm did—and maybe he'd be tossed overboard by the force of the storm. The clumsy pirate gave Carolina a half-hearted wave.

She climbed up to the foredeck, taking deep breaths to clear the stale ship air from her lungs. She leaned against the rail at the prow of the ship, imagining the day when she would be a pirate captain herself, sailing the seas, liberating treasure from Spanish ships, and fighting villains such as the East India Trading Company. Her favorite daydream was that one day she'd capture a ship and find the cruel old governor she was once supposed to marry on board. He'd be horrified and beg on his knees for mercy, and she would laugh and laugh before leaving him on a beach somewhere—somewhere his soldiers could eventually find him, so they'd laugh at him, too.

Normally this daydream included Diego as her first mate, but after she saw him kissing Marcella in India, she'd thrown him off her imaginary ship. She hated to think that her mother might be right—that boys wanted girls who acted like true princesses. She'd thought at least Diego was different . . . but apparently not. Well, if he wanted a girl who wore pretty dresses and loved tea and embroidery, then fine; that certainly wasn't going to be her. If that's what he wanted, then he deserved Marcella.

She brushed at her cheek angrily, telling herself it was just raindrops she was wiping away.

That's when she noticed the rain was stopping. Carolina held out her hand and watched the drops slow to a drizzle. A ray of sunlight suddenly broke through the heavy cloud cover, and she saw a glimmer of blue in the ocean below her. She wanted to whoop with joy. Finally, the end of the storm!

"Land!" Diego shouted from the crow's nest. "Land ho! Dead ahead!"

"Aaaah!" Catastrophe Shane yelped, grabbing the wheel. He spun it one way and then the other, and the *Pearl* listed perilously.

Carolina jumped down from the foredeck and ran back to the wheel, pushing Shane aside. She could see the land ahead of them now, too: dark green hills and thick jungles emerging from the fog along the white sandy beaches.

Emerging *fast*.

She gripped the wheel and hauled on it, praying that there weren't any rocks hiding in wait for them.

"Carolina," Diego called, swinging down

through the ratlines. She wanted to ignore him, but she knew she had to listen for the sake of the ship. "There's a bay ahead," he shouted. "If you sail between those spurs of land, we might be able to drop anchor there for a day or two to resupply."

"Oi," Jack said indignantly, popping his head out of his cabin. "Who's the captain here, eh?"

"Sorry, Jack," Diego said. He landed on a crossbeam and stopped, clinging to the ropes. He pointed to the land ahead of them. "I was just saying—"

"I'm not deaf, lad," Jack said. "But I *am* the captain. As such, I give the orders around here, savvy? Carolina!"

"Yes, sir?"

"Steer us between those spurs of land. We'll drop anchor in that bay and resupply."

"Yes, sir!" Carolina called.

"But that's what—" Diego started, and then

he stopped himself. "Very good idea, sir."

Pirates began clambering up from below-decks, yelling about the land and the end of the storm, as Jack strode over to stand beside Carolina. He pulled out his spyglass and squinted at the long, green shore ahead of them.

"Hmm," he said. "This looks horribly familiar."

"Is it Africa?" Carolina asked eagerly. "Will we see more elephants?"

"Blimey, I hope not," Jack said. He tapped the end of his spyglass against his teeth. "No. What are the chances we—it can't be."

A few of the pirates were dancing on the deck, exulting in the fresh air and faint rays of sunlight. Barbossa stomped out of Jack's cabin and stopped them by thrusting mops and buckets into their hands. "The deck could use a good swabbin', ye lazy sots," he growled.

"Look!" Diego shouted, pointing. The *Pearl* was sailing into an enormous, gleaming blue bay. The water here was calm and clear, and they could see huge-eyed monkeys with ringed tails watching the pirate ship from the trees. And then there was the collection of buildings that Diego was pointing at. "There's a settlement of some kind—a town!"

"A well-guarded town," Billy observed. On either side of the harbor, on the bits of land jutting out into the bay, stood an eight-sided fort built of thick wood, bristling with cannons and guns—all of them pointed at the *Pearl*. More cannons were lined up along the water's edge. And a fierce-looking crowd was already gathering at the dock, waiting for them. Most of them held swords or daggers or pistols, or, in some cases, all three. Several of them had long scars or missing teeth or eye patches, and, Jack noticed, a few had hats that were nearly as excellent as his.

"Not to worry," he announced to his crew.

"I'll just have a chat with these lovely gents and—uh-oh."

Carolina followed his gaze to the black flag that rippled over the town's largest building. On it, a white skeleton and a pirate were depicted holding an hourglass between them, with a dripping heart below it. It was a Jolly Roger she'd never seen before.

"Not good," Jack said, seizing the wheel and bumping Carolina out of the way. "Not good, not good, not good."

Barbossa whirled around and spotted the flag as well. His jaw dropped. "It's Libertalia!" he bellowed.

"Libertalia?" Billy said. "I thought that was just a legend."

"It is!" Jack said eagerly. "Absolutely a legend! No such thing. Certainly not right there in front of us. Better we be off, then."

Barbossa bounded over to the wheel and

seized a spoke opposite the one Jack held, stopping him from turning the ship. "Jack, are you mad? Never mind, don't bother answering that. This is the perfect place to stop."

"Aye," Billy agreed. "He's right, Jack. If it really is Libertalia."

"What's Libertalia?" Diego asked. Carolina had never heard of it either. She looked curiously at Jack's alarmed expression.

"A perfectly imaginary place," Jack said. "Right, off we go, gold to acquire, bad guys to avoid."

"You seem awfully spooked by this 'imaginary' place," Carolina pointed out.

"Libertalia is a pirate utopia," Jean answered, leaning on the rail as if he were thinking of jumping overboard to swim to the town. "A place where pirates live in harmony and safety after they've retired from their lives of plunder. It was founded by the infamous Captain Misson many years ago. Pirates all over the world tell stories about it. And here it really is, in front of us!"

"Ha," Jack muttered. "'Retired.' As if pirates ever do that."

"Maybe Lakshmi and I could live here once she's free," Jean said with a dreamy expression. Lakshmi was a warrior who had been assigned to watch Jack while he was in Sri Sumbhajee's palace. Instead, she had fallen in love with Jean—and vice versa—and he had promised to return for her after the final battle with the Shadow Lord, when her debt to the Indian Pirate Lord would finally be repaid.*

"We have to resupply, Jack," Barbossa insisted.

"And fix the ship," Diego said, pointing to a huge crack in the mainmast and the tattered

*We met her in Vol. 3, *The Turning Tide*

black sails, which had been shredded by the storm.

"And *eat something*," Jean said urgently.

"Fortune has clearly brought us here," Barbossa said, waving his hand around at the bay.

"Felt more like a horrible, wet, nasty storm than fortune to *me*," Jack said. "We're going to regret this," Jack muttered under his breath as he sighed and steered up to the dock.

"Cheer up, Jack," said Carolina. "This is probably the perfect place to learn more about the Pirate Lord of the Atlantic Ocean. Maybe we can even find him here! Or *her*," she added quickly.

"That would be a little obvious," Jack said snidely. "The Pirate Lord living a life of ease in Libertalia? Doubtful."

"Look at all the pirates!" Carolina said, awestruck by the range of characters lined up along the dock. She could see faces from all around the world—Indian, Arabic, Dutch, French, English, Chinese, and most numerous of all, African.

"The legend of Libertalia says that the pirates here are famous for attacking ships as they leave Africa loaded with slaves. The slaves are all freed and offered the chance to live here as free men," Billy explained to her.

"*Maravilloso*," she said, her eyes shining.

"Oh, don't you get all sappy about this place. It's not all noble deeds and heroic heroism," Jack scoffed. "They are still *pirates*. There's a lot of looting and pillaging for treasure, too."

"You mean like normal pirates?" Barbossa grumbled. "Attacking ships instead of haring around the world on a vague, loony mission? Sounds bloody perfect."

The anchor thudded into the sand below them, and Jack led the way to the gangplank.

His eyes roamed the crowd, and Carolina realized he was looking for someone. Knowing Jack, she expected a couple of angry women to come storming up and slap him at any second.

So she was surprised when the pirates all stepped back and made way for a tall, thin older man in a long crimson frock coat, heavy with silver embroidery. His hair was dark and curly, held back by a green bandanna. Gold gleamed in his teeth and on his fingers. Sharp eyes peered over his prominent nose and matted goatee. He stopped at the bottom of the gangplank and grinned up at the *Pearl*'s captain.

"Jackie," he said. "Now this is quite a surprise. Come to visit your old man at last, have you?"

CHAPTER THREE

All the pirates on the *Black Pearl* goggled at Jack and the man on the dock.

"Is that—did he just—" Jean sputtered.

"Did he call you *Jackie*?" Barbossa said with enormous glee.

"Crew, meet Captain Teague," Jack said through gritted teeth.

"Lord of Madagascar," Teague said grandly, sweeping his bicorne hat off his head in an elegant bow. Carolina could see where Jack got his flamboyance from. "That's me. And what lucky wind brings you to Libertalia, Jackie? In need of rescuing, as usual?"

"Not at all," Jack said, drawing himself up tall. "As you can see, I am the captain of this magnificent ship—which is mine, I might add, all my own—and I am not in need of any rescue at all!"

"Except for that whole Shadow-Lord-chasing-you thing," Barbossa pointed out.

Teague's eyebrows went up.

"Nothing! Ignore him!" Jack shouted. "We are just here to resupply, and then we'll be on our merry way. Lots of fierce piratey things to do out there. We're very busy with all the, uh, looting. And the plundering, of course. With a bit of ransacking and a doddle of pillaging thrown in."

Captain Teague eyed the *Black Pearl* up and down. "Well, Jackie, I must say, you have got yourself a fine ship here. Much better than that one you started out with. What was that leaky old bucket called?"

"The *Barnacle*!" Jean cried, starting to laugh. He remembered sailing the Caribbean with Jack Sparrow and their friends Arabella and Tumen when they were younger.*

"Yes, ha-ha-ha," Jack said, infuriated. "I'll have you know the *Barnacle* was a fantastic—well, great—well, seaworthy—for the most part—respectable boat, and it would have served me well for many more years if *you* hadn't gotten it blown up by the Royal Navy," he snapped at Teague.

"You should thank me," Teague said calmly, eyeing the *Pearl*. "You've evidently moved up in the world. I wonder how long this one will last you."

"None of your beeswax," Jack said. "Now, if

*As recounted in the series *Pirates of the Caribbean: Jack Sparrow* you'll excuse us, we have some bartering to do." He waved Barbossa forward and started down the gangplank as if he intended to march right past Teague.

But the old pirate put his arm out and stopped Jack in his tracks. His craggy face creased as he examined Jack's face.

"Still wearing too much eyeliner, I see," he said disapprovingly.

"Listen, when *you're* captain of the fastest ship in the world, perhaps we can have a conversation about my fashion choices," Jack snapped. "Until then, adieu." He lifted his hat in a farewell salute.

But Teague still wasn't moving. And until he moved, none of the pirates behind him were going to let Jack get by them either.

"Jackie," Teague said with a thin smile, "the least you could do is stop by and say hello to the family."

"Now *why* would I want to do that?" Jack asked. "Years ago, I ran away from home precisely to get away from that 'family,' remember? And you, I might add."

"Now, Jackie," Teague admonished, "your grandmother would be so delighted to see you."

"No, she wouldn't," Jack pointed out. "She'll probably try to kill me. Again."

"Well, probably," Teague agreed. He fingered one of the long braids in his beard, squinting cannily. "But just think what she'll do if she finds out you were here and *didn't* say hello."

Jack thought about that for a moment and shivered.

"Come back to the mansion and stay with us for the night," Teague said. "I insist. You can even bring some of your crew with you. That bonny one up there, perhaps." He pointed at Carolina.

Up on the deck of the *Pearl*, Diego scowled as jealousy flared in his chest. He wished he could go over and put his arm around Carolina, to let this tall, imposing pirate know that she was already taken . . . but of course, she wasn't really, since she refused to even acknowledge Diego's existence at the moment.

Jack sighed heavily. "Fine," he said. "Carolina, Diego, Barbossa, and Jean with me. Billy, you round up the other pirates and take care of business in Libertalia. Try not to lose any of 'em—I know how pirates can get once they see this place."

"Oh, no, you don't!" Jack flinched as Marcella flounced down the gangplank. "You're not leaving me with these horrible beasts! Where Diego goes, I go! Especially if there might be dinner with proper silverware and linen napkins involved." She batted her eyelashes at Teague, who looked mildly horrified.

"Might as well say yes," Jack said to him, secretly pleased that at least he could inflict some pain on Teague in return. "She doesn't take well to being told no."

"Did I hear you say you're a lord?" Marcella said to Teague. She wove her arm through his and gave his elegant coat an admiring look.

"Bad news, lass," Jack said, enjoying the expression on Teague's face. "He's a lord of *pirates.*"

"Oh!" she squeaked, jumping away from Teague.

Jack beckoned Billy over to him and lowered his voice, but the Libertalia pirates were pressing in close, and he could see Teague watching him curiously.

"Billy," he said quietly, "see if you can find out anything about that . . . *person* . . . you know, the one we have a vested interest in finding?"

"Who, you mean the Pirate Lord of the Atlantic Ocean?" Billy said, evidently completely missing the point of Jack's lowered voice.

A hiss swept through the crowd, and suddenly the pirates looked ten times more hostile than before, which Jack wouldn't have thought possible.

"What!" he said in an exaggeratedly loud voice. "Who? Never heard of him! No! Certainly not! Couldn't care less about the fellow!" He winked hugely at Billy, hoping his old friend would interpret correctly.

Unfortunately for Jack, Billy was used to seeing Jack do lots of peculiar things, so he had long since given up on figuring out the meaning of any of them.

"But I thought you wanted us to find him," Billy said blankly. "That's the whole reason we're here, isn't it?"

Now the pirates of Libertalia were practically growling. Jack slapped his forehead and looked pained.

"See, this is the problem with pirates," he said.

"Not great communicators, I'm afraid. With the notable exception of myself, of course."

"You'll not find that bloody Pirate Lord here!" shouted a one-legged man in the crowd.

"If we caught a whiff of 'im near Libertalia, we'd skin him alive and play music with his bones!" yelled another pirate.

"And cut off his toes!" bellowed a third.

"And feed his flesh to our cattle!"

Jack wrinkled his nose. "First of all, what kind of self-respecting pirates have cattle? And secondly, while I applaud your creativity when it comes to violence, I do have to wonder why any pirate wouldn't be welcome in a pirate utopia?"

"King Samuel is a liar and a traitor!" snarled an African pirate with two gold teeth and a long scar along his well-muscled shoulder.

"King Samuel," Jack muttered out of the corner of his mouth to Billy. "Remember that." He turned back to the pirate who had spoken.

"A liar and a traitor, eh? Sounds horribly like . . . a *pirate*." He widened his eyes thoughtfully.

"But this one doesn't honor the Code!" The scarred pirate slammed his fist into the palm of his other hand. "He's made underhanded deals with the Dutch and the Portuguese to let their slave ships through. He's been selling people— prisoners he captures, warriors he defeats, even his own people!—as slaves. He calls himself a king . . . but the truth is, he is nothing but filth." The man spat in the dirt.

Jack frowned. He himself had some fairly strong feelings about selling people—namely, that it was utterly wrong. Not to mention unworthy of a pirate. But he had no choice; he needed to find this King Samuel to retrieve his vial of Shadow Gold.

And yet, how could he Parlay with a man like that? Accepting hospitality from Sri Sumbhajee was one thing; this was quite another. Clearly this would be a very different kind of mission from the first few.

"That's horrible!" Carolina gasped. Jack realized she and Diego had come down from the ship and were standing behind him. "Jack," she said, "we shouldn't have anything to do with a dishonorable pirate like that. He won't help us against the Shadow Lord—nor would we want his help!"

"Shadow Lord?" Teague echoed curiously.

"You might be right," Jack said to Carolina, "but that's not the only business we have with the Pirate Lord, remember?" He gave her a significant look, and unlike Billy, she got the hint and stopped talking.

"Well, as you can see, Jackie, you'll not find much love for King Samuel around these parts," Teague observed. He glanced slyly at the *Black Pearl*. "Perhaps if you told me what you were looking for . . ."

"No," Jack said stoutly. "I'll take care of it myself."

"Hmmm," Teague said, narrowing his eyes. After a long pause he continued, "Very well. To the mansion, then . . . Grandmama awaits." He grinned crookedly and turned with a flourish of his red coat.

Jack shuddered. The truth was, he would much rather do battle with King Samuel, or even face the Shadow Lord all by himself, then go home with Teague to have dinner with his grandmother.

But he had no choice. Lifting his chin, he led his motley crew through the crowd as the Libertalia pirates parted respectfully for Captain Teague.

He just hoped they wouldn't be serving that disgusting cod soup he remembered from his childhood.

CHAPTER FOUR

Captain Teague lived in the largest house in Libertalia—a three-story mansion built of mahogany and other strong jungle woods. The polished dark brown walls and bronze accents gleamed in the long rays of the sunset. Jack eyed the windows suspiciously as he approached. He was sure there were family members lurking behind each of them, watching him walk up with his crew and probably planning something sinister.

One family member wasn't bothering to hide. She sat in an ebony rocking chair on the large veranda that ran around the front of the house. Her sharp black eyes glared out from a spiderweb of deep wrinkles. The chair went thump-*thump* on the boards of the veranda as she rocked vigorously back and forth. A bright red bandanna covered her thick gray curls, and Jack knew that the false teeth she wore included two of gold and one with a small ruby set in it. As a child, that ruby had given him nightmares. To him, it always looked as if she had a spot of blood on her teeth, left there after she ate her enemies.

"Grandmama," Jack said, lifting his hat to her at the foot of the porch stairs. "Looking well as always. Better than I expected. Rather surprised to see you still alive, in fact."

His grandmother snorted. "Not as surprised as I am to see *you* still alive," she snapped. "You must be as lucky as you are stupid."

Barbossa snickered, then quickly put on a bland expression when Jack turned to glare at him.

Grandmama's voice was as strong and husky as ever. She had been eighty-two when Jack left home as a teenager. Several years had passed since then, and she didn't look a day older. Jack's eyes went to the wrinkled hands that clutched her gleaming wooden cane. He knew from painful experience that there was a very sharp sword hidden inside that cane, not to mention the daggers she kept tucked away in various pockets of her attire.

"Why don't you introduce us to your crew?" Teague interceded smoothly.

"Right," Jack said. "This is my first mate, Hector Barbossa—bit of an odd duck. Has a thing for feathers, as you can see. Don't mind the dreadful hat."

"I can *hear* you," Barbossa growled at him.

"I quite like the hat," Grandmama said, giving Barbossa a suggestive smile. He squinted off at the setting sun, pretending not to notice.

"Jean Magliore, my Creole friend from my *Barnacle* days," Jack went on, waving his hand at the redheaded sailor. "His cousin Marcella, and our star-crossed lovers, Diego de Leon and Princess Carolina of Spain. I, of course, am the captain. Everyone may address me as Captain Jack."

"Very impressive, Jackie," Teague said, and Jack frowned at him. Carolina and Diego both turned red and avoided each other's eyes.

"HEY," Marcella said loudly. "I'm a star-crossed lover, too! It's *me* and Diego, not him and Carolina! Get your facts straight, Sparrow!"

Grandmama's eyebrows went up, and her chair thumped faster on the porch floorboards. "You let your crew talk to you like that?" she sneered at Jack.

"I'm not part of his crew!" Marcella shouted before Jack could answer. She tossed her lanky blond hair back. "I'm not a pirate! I'm a lady! A—an honored guest! Taken against my will!"

Carolina rolled her eyes, and Grandmama chuckled in a faintly sinister way. "That is how we get most of our honored guests," the old lady mused.

"Shall we go in to supper?" Teague suggested. He held the door open and shepherded the guests inside. Grandmama heaved herself to her feet and followed, thumping pointedly with her cane. Jack barely managed to dodge it before she brought it down on his toes.

The front door opened into a surprisingly grand hall, open all the way to the roof, with a vast staircase spiraling around the walls to the upper two stories. Rich Oriental carpets woven in deep reds and browns and gold—no doubt plundered from some treasure-laden trading vessel—were spread across the floors and stairs.

Teague ushered them to the left, into a dining room with tall windows along two sides. Through them, the pirates could see that night had fallen outside. Several closed doors along the third wall led to other parts of the house. Candles flickered on the long table and shining bronze lamps hung down from the ceiling, casting a warm glow.

"Ooooooooooh," Marcella said, clasping her hands together at the sight of the white damask tablecloth. "Linen! Silverware! It's so civilized!"

"Yes," Jack said. "Very civilized stolen tablecloths and plundered forks."

Marcella ignored him. It had been long enough since she saw a properly laid table that she was willing to ignore where it all came from. "*This* is *much* nicer than sitting on the floor to eat your dinner, I *must* say," she said rapturously, feeling the tablecloth between her fingers. "Plus there aren't any horrible monkeys to steal your jewelry."

Teague gave Jack a questioning look.

"Nothing," Jack said quickly. He spun his finger by his temple meaningfully. "Raving, she is. Quite sad, really."

"Sitting on the floor," Grandmama muttered, stomping over to the large chair at the nearest end of the table. "Monkeys." She sat down and pointed her cane at Jack. "You've been to Sri Sumbhajee's palace."

Diego's jaw dropped. How had she guessed? Jack looked disgruntled.

"Ah. Visiting Pirate Lords, are you?" Teague said, stroking his beard. He sat down at the other end of the table and motioned for Jack to sit to his right. The others pulled out chairs and sat down, jostling each other as they fought silently not to get stuck next to Grandmama. In the end, Carolina sat on one side of her with

Barbossa on the other. Diego was across from Jack, with Marcella between him and Carolina, and Jean sat between Jack and Barbossa.

"What do you want with the Pirate Lords, Jackie?" Teague asked. He rang a small silver bell that was beside him on the table.

"Just seeing the world," Jack said airily. "Visiting old acquaintances. Making some new ones. Are those new salt shakers?" Trying to distract Teague from the subject of his travels, he picked up one of the egg-shaped silver things on the table and nearly poured pepper in his eye as he examined it. A pair of servants appeared through one of the doors and began laying out platters of food—including roast beef, yams, and several intriguing and unfamiliar vegetables. Jean's stomach growled loud enough for everyone to hear.

"Here you go, Jackie," Teague said, pouring a thick white liquid from a tureen into a bowl and setting it in front of him. "Cod soup! Your favorite!"

Jack poked the soup glumly with his spoon.

"Huh," Grandmama snorted again. She pointed at Jack. "You know, the Brethren Court has gone way downhill since *my* day."

"Your day?" Carolina said. "Did you know earlier Pirate Lords of the Brethren Court?"

"KNOW THEM?" Grandmama bellowed, her face turning purple with anger. "I WAS a Pirate Lord of the Brethren Court, you ignorant hussy!"

"You *were*?" Carolina breathed. Female pirate captains were her heroes. She'd nearly died of excitement when she met Mistress Ching, Pirate Lord of the Pacific. She couldn't believe she'd sailed with Jack all this time and he'd never mentioned that he had a famous pirate grandmother. "That's amazing!"

Carolina's expression of genuine awe seemed

to mollify Grandmama a bit. "Oh, yes," she said. "Pirate Lord of the whole Atlantic Ocean, me. I was present for the second meeting of the court, where Morgan and Bartholomew set out the Pirate Code. Youngest Pirate Lord ever, I was. And the prettiest."

"Until me," Jack observed as he speared a chunk of beef onto his plate.

Grandmama gave him a steely glare. "I am *still* prettier than you. And a much better pirate."

Jack waggled his fork at her. "Ah, but being that I am the one in possession of a ship and crew, and not only that but the *finest* and fastest ship in all the world, I think the question of superior piratical skills might be up for debate."

"So what were Morgan and Bartholomew like?" Diego said quickly, hoping to stave off that particular "debate," especially since it seemed likely to involve Grandmama flinging tankards and possibly knives.

"Oh, don't get her started," Jack moaned, but it was too late.

"Bartholomew was everything a pirate should be," Grandmama said wistfully. "Fierce, quick to anger, violent, conniving, the whole package. He used to stick burning brands in his long black beard when he fought, so it looked like his whole head was smoking. Scared the devil out of the cowards he attacked. He was as tall as a house with shoulders as wide as four trees and the thickest, blackest eyebrows the world has ever seen. I never saw him smile, not once. Now *there* was a real pirate." She gave Jack a look that clearly said "unlike *you*."

"Morgan, on the other hand, was a pretty useless pirate," she went on, loading her plate with yams. "Kept losing his charts or dropping his compass over the side by accident, that sort of thing. But he had a flair for words. He's the one that gave the Code its character. And rumor had it that he used that brain of his for some pretty nasty plans here and there, at least until he settled down to be governor of Jamaica, the lazy sot. Ah, well. I'm the only one from that court who's still alive." She cackled. "Outlasted all the old goats, I did."

"Well, it helps that you've retired to a pirate utopia," Jack pointed out. "There's not too many folks here trying to poke you with sharp, pointy things, are there?"

Quick as a flash, Grandmama seized her steak knife and hurled it at Jack's head. He just managed to dodge out of the way, nearly falling out of his chair in the process.

"Now, Grandmama," Teague said calmly. "No violence until after the soup course, please."

She scowled at Jack. "I'm still planning to go out fighting, with a sword in my hand. See if I don't!" she snapped.

"I would much rather *not* be there to see that," Jack said sincerely. "Since I imagine I'll be the one you're trying to stick with it."

"You better believe it," Grandmama grumbled, stabbing her peas viciously.

"I want to know everything," Carolina said, her eyes shining. "What was your ship called? Where did you sail? Did you—"

But Carolina's questions were not to be answered—for at that very moment, the sound of shattering glass suddenly filled the room. Figures in dark clothes crashed through the windows, brandishing long swords and deadly looking cutlasses. Jack only caught a glimpse of malevolent eyes bearing down on him before the wind from outside swept through the room, blowing out the candles and lamps.

They were under attack—and they were fighting in pitch darkness!

CHAPTER FIVE

In one fluid movement, Jack drew his sword with one hand and seized his chair with the other, whipping it around in front of him like a shield. He heard a loud *OOF*! as someone stumbled into one of the chair legs. He shoved the chair into the person's chest, and whirled his sword around—but stopped short. What if he was slashing at the wrong person? What if he accidentally stabbed Barbossa or Diego instead of one of their attackers?

Eh, no big loss, he thought.

He stood still for a moment, listening to the crashes and shouts echoing around him in the darkness and trying to gauge how many attackers there were. They made very little noise as they fought—certainly not as much as Jack's crew. Clearly, Captain Teague had no qualms about who he might hit; Jack could hear the all-too-familiar sound of Teague's huge sword clanging against others and the deep chuckle Teague always let out when he struck flesh.

On the other side of the table, Diego jumped to his feet as the lights went out. He reached wildly around him, only one thought flashing through his head. Carolina! I must get her to safety!

Long hair brushed through his fingers. He seized her shoulders and she let out a yelp of surprise.

"Don't argue with me!" he whispered. "Quickly! We must hide!"

He felt her start to pull away, so he wrapped his arms around her, picked her up, and carried her over to the doors in the opposite wall. Clanging swords crashed close to his head and he stumbled, banging his shin on a tipped-over chair. The girl in his arms nearly struggled loose, but he managed to grip her wrist and yank her after him through the first door his groping hand found. He slammed it behind them before he realized it led to a closet, small and dark. But that didn't matter—at least they were safe! To his surprise, he felt Carolina throw her arms around his neck gratefully, and his lips met hers in the dark.

Out in the pirate-filled dining room, Barbossa fought with canny instinct, sensing each attack and darting out of the way. He wondered where Jack was in the dark room. A thought crossed his mind: if Jack somehow ended up on the wrong end of a sword . . . In this darkness, nobody need know who did it. And then the *Pearl* would be his! He began to move stealthily around the table to where he thought he'd last seen his captain.

Meanwhile, Jack reached into the dark with his sword hand and felt the edge of the table beside him. He quickly clambered onto it, slipping a little on the sheer tablecloth. He winced as his boots landed on someone's plate and yams squished underfoot. But it couldn't be helped—being up on the table would give him a position of strength. And besides, this was an excellent opportunity to get rid of the cod soup. He calculated carefully, and then aimed a ferocious kick at the soup tureen. It went flying off the table and someone hollered unhappily as soup splashed all over them.

Pleased, Jack heaved his chair up after him and began whacking it from side to side. He could hear grunts of pain as it connected with pirate heads on either side of the table.

"YEE-HAAAA!" Jack heard Grandmama shriek with excitement. "Take that, you scoundrels! Break into *my* house, will you? Think an old lady can't defend herself? How do you like the taste of that dagger, eh? I've got ten more! Come and get 'em!"

Jack was sorely tempted to aim his chair in the direction of her voice, but somehow he was sure she would know it was him, even in the dark. And he had no desire to meet her daggers—he'd run afoul of them quite enough as a young lad.

Something whizzed past his ear and he ducked, wondering what Grandmama was throwing now.

Who was attacking them? The enemy fought in eerie silence, melting in and out of the shadows. Every "oof!" and "OW!" Jack heard sounded as if it came from his own crew. Who were these dangerous, powerful fighters that had struck so suddenly?

Was it Benedict's army, back again? Surely they couldn't have caught up to the *Pearl* so quickly. Not only that, but the Royal Navy tended to be a lot noisier about their battles. Lots of clanking and pistols and yelling orders and so on.

Suddenly, Jack felt a hand clamp around his boot. Startled, he whipped his other foot around and kicked his assailant in the face with a loud crunching sound. The hand released him and he heard a thud as the person hit the floor. "Sorry," he called over the battle sounds, hoping it wasn't a friend he'd just whacked (he wouldn't mind if it were family).

What if these were King Samuel's men? Jack ducked as something else flew over his head. He danced across the table, trying to tiptoe around the food platters while knocking pirates over the head as he went. Why would King Samuel be attacking Captain Teague's house? Perhaps he'd heard that another Pirate Lord was here and wanted to test his mettle. Jack preened for a second before realizing that didn't make much sense—again, how would he have gotten here so quickly?

Then something tugged on Jack's long dreadlocks, and he felt a stab of fear in his gut. Worst of all . . . what if they were being attacked by the Shadow Lord? He could be anywhere, anytime, as far as Jack knew, and it made sense that his army would prefer to fight in darkness. Perhaps these were his deadly shadow warriors, sent to stop Jack before he could find another vial of Shadow Gold.

Jack remembered the carnage they'd seen in Panama*—the smoking town and lifeless bodies left behind after the Shadow Army attacked.

*In Vol. 1: *The Caribbean*

From what Alex said, it sounded as if they could appear and disappear like smoke, destroying everything in their path.

His heart hammered in his chest, and he took a careful step back to the center of the table. Whoever they were fighting, he had his own demons to fight as well. His shadow-sickness always got worse in the dark, as the shadows gathered gleefully to pull on his braids and clamber along his coat. His shoulders felt heavier and heavier, weighed down by the shadows piling onto his back. Nausea built up in his stomach, and he fought a wave of panic.

Jack took another step back, away from the fighting, and felt something solid brush against his shoulder. He jumped and flailed and nearly sliced his sword through it before he realized what it was . . . one of the bronze lamps hanging from the ceiling over the table.

An idea struck him. If they were fighting

shadows, what better to fight them with than light? Or at least they could get a look at who they were dealing with. It would be nice to know if he was kicking his own people in the face.

Jack threw the chair in his hand out into the room, where it landed on someone who yelped in pain. He fumbled through his coat, searching for a tinderbox. He knew he had one somewhere in his pockets . . . no, that was his folding spyglass . . . a handful of gold coins . . . something that felt like a hairball—where had *that* come from?—and then, finally . . .

"Aha!" he cried in delight, whisking the tinderbox out of his pocket. Quick as a wink, a flame flared between his hands and he set the oil of the lamp ablaze. In just a few steps he was able to do the same to the other two lamps.

As light filled the room, all the battling pirates stopped fighting and shielded their eyes for a moment. Blinking, they looked around in surprise.

They were not fighting shadows after all. The fierce strangers who had burst through the windows were men—tall, muscular men with long daggers and very piratical outfits. Jack squinted. A few of them looked oddly familiar.

"Jack Sparrow?" said a voice behind him.

Jack whirled and spotted the leader of the attack. His mouth dropped open.

"Gombo!"

CHAPTER SIX

Back at the beginning of his adventure with the Shadow Gold, Jack had helped a runaway slave named Gombo escape from New Orleans by giving him passage on the *Pearl*. Gombo had later left the ship to captain his own crew, but Jack hadn't expected to find him here—certainly not at the other end of his sword!

The tall pirate captain gave Jack a stern look. "It's Gentleman Jocard now," he said. "Not Gombo anymore. You must remember that."

Then suddenly he broke into a wide smile. "Hello, Jack."

"*Captain* Jack," Jack reminded him, delighted to see his old friend. "How are you? Sick of captaining your own ship by now, eh?" he asked hopefully, sheathing his sword. "You must be ready to come back and be our cook again. Well, tell you what, agree to a pay cut—half your wages, say—and I'll think about it, savvy?"

"What wages?" Jean asked ruefully, rubbing a lump that was forming on his head. Jack winced guiltily.

"Thanks for the offer, Jack," Jocard said, amused, "but I'm afraid life aboard the *Ranger* suits me very well."

All the pirates jumped as loud thumping noises echoed through the room. Jack glanced around at his pirates. Teague and Grandmama were at either end of the table, still brandishing their weapons. Barbossa was staggering to his feet with a furious expression, cod soup dripping from his hair and blood dripping from his nose. Uh-oh, Jack thought, noticing the fierce glare Barbossa was directing at Jack's boots.

And Carolina was standing with her back to the wall, sword in hand, facing three of Jocard's pirates. She glanced around as Jack did, frowning quizzically.

Someone was missing . . . *two* someones.

THUMP, THUMP, THUMP!

"Help!" cried a muffled voice.

Carolina strode over to a door in the side wall and threw it open, revealing a small closet—and Diego and Marcella!

Marcella had her arms around a flustered Diego, while he was struggling to get away. He'd realized his mistake moments after the door closed. In the dark, he'd grabbed the wrong girl! Of course, there was no telling Marcella that; she was convinced that he was her savior.

"Wait!" Diego cried, seeing Carolina. "I didn't—this isn't what it looks like! It was an accident!"

Carolina gave him a disgusted look and strode over to stand beside Jack, resolutely turning her back on Diego.

"Oh, it's *you*," Marcella said, spotting Jocard. She disentangled herself from Diego and sauntered into the room, fluffing her hair. "What an unpleasant surprise. I thought we'd finally gotten rid of you."

"If I had known *you'd* be here," Jocard said to her, folding his arms, "I never would have come."

"Now there's a sentiment I can agree with," Jack said heartily.

Marcella stuck out her tongue at Jocard.

"Gentleman Jocard," Teague said thoughtfully. He twirled his sword in his fingers, clearly not willing to sheath it yet. "I've heard much of you. In only a few short months, I hear, you have become one of the most prosperous and respected pirates in the waters around Libertalia."

Jocard gave a small bow of acknowledgment, and Marcella rolled her eyes. "Ooooh, aren't you *fancy*," she snipped. "La la la, sooooo good at being a *pirate*, like *that's* anything to brag about."

"At least I am good at something," Jocard said gravely, "unlike certain people, who are good for nothing but whining and eating nine times their weight in food."

Marcella gasped with outrage. "Diego!" she cried. "Defend me!"

"Ahem," Teague said, clearing his throat. "If I may interrupt this touching reunion—would anyone mind explaining *why* you were attacking *my* mansion?"

Jocard gestured to his pirates, motioning for them to stand down. Daggers vanished under shirts and into boots; Jack saw at least two men slip their weapons into their hats. Suddenly the room seemed a lot less troublesome. Jack jumped off the table and wiped yams off his boots onto the carpet, until Grandmama gave him a beady-eyed stare and he stopped, trying to look innocent.

"I heard that you were entertaining a Pirate Lord," Jocard said to Captain Teague. "I assumed it was King Samuel . . . but I am most pleased to discover that I was wrong." The corners of his mouth twitched as he glanced at Jack. "Of all the Pirate Lords—I must admit you were the last I would have expected to find here, Jack."

"Oh, me, too, mate," Jack said fervently. "Would love to be a thousand miles from here, if I could. No offense," he said to Teague, who shrugged.

"So," Jack went on, studying Jocard's fierce,

proud expression. "You have a problem with King Samuel, eh?"

All the pirates in Jocard's crew scowled, and Jocard's face darkened. "He must be stopped," the captain said in a low, passionate voice. Something in his tone hinted at a personal vendetta, but when he didn't elaborate, Jack decided not to press it.

"Well," he said, "it just so happens that we're looking for this Samuel fellow ourselves." Jack tapped his nose, thinking.

"We should look for him together!" Carolina burst out. "And fight him together! We can stop him, I know we can!"

"I say!" Jack gave her an outraged look. "What did I say about who the captain is around here? It's me, that's who! I give the orders, savvy?"

"Yes, I know," Carolina said. "But—"

"Ah, ah, ah!" Jack said. "No buts! Shush! I

have a fantastic idea!" He turned to Jocard. "We should fight King Samuel together! Strength in numbers, eh?"

Carolina sighed.

"You with all your brawny pirates," Jack went on, "and me with my brains and cunning and savoir faire and exceptional fashion sense. I think this could work."

"No way!" Marcella complained. "This cold-hearted *pirate* abandoned us! I don't want to work with him! Make him go away!"

"Interesting," Jocard said, ignoring her. "Pirates working together—most unorthodox."

As they were speaking, Teague drew his chair out from the table and sat down, flinging his coattails out behind him regally. He lifted his eyebrow at the food on the table, most of it now clearly covered in Jack's bootprints, and rang the small silver bell again. As servants hurried in quietly to clear the table, Teague folded his hands in front of him and regarded Jack and Jocard.

"What you are proposing is very unwise," Teague said darkly. "King Samuel is impossible to defeat. Don't you think I would have done it myself otherwise?"

"Not necessarily," Grandmama said from the other end of the table. She grabbed a hunk of beef off one of the untrampled platters before the servants took it away and started gnawing on it with gusto. "You're not as daring as you used to be, my boy. Now, if *I* were still running things, no one else would *dare* call themselves king around here!"

Teague gave her an unpleasant look and turned back to Jack. "If you do this," he said, "and if you fail, which I am certain you will, King Samuel will seek revenge on all the pirates here. I guarantee he will attack Libertalia and destroy it. I have no love for Samuel myself, but at least right now we have an uneasy truce. We leave each other alone. You break that truce—and many will suffer for it."

"Many *are* suffering!" Jocard cried, slamming his hand on the table. "Every day King Samuel allows more and more of our people to be sold into slavery. We cannot stand by and let him go on like this!"

"Besides," Jack pointed out, "he is a pirate, remember. Which means he could change his mind at any moment and come charging over here with his slave-trading ships ready and waiting for new cargo."

"Exactly," Jocard said. "We overthrow Samuel, and then a better Pirate Lord of the Atlantic Ocean can ensure the safety of Libertalia for a long time to come."

Teague snorted. "Easier said than done. King Samuel's fortress is south of here, on the western side of Madagascar, on a cliff high above the sea.

It is impossible to scale. A thicket of warships waits in the bay below, and cannons line the shore. You'll never even get close enough to shout a feeble threat before you find yourselves at the bottom of the sea. I'm certainly not joining you on this foolhardy mission."

"Tut, tut," Jack said, waving one hand dismissively. "Leave all the planning to me! I'll do the thinking, Jocard will do the fighting. Sounds perfectly fair."

"Hmmm," Jocard responded. He stroked his beard and studied Jack. "We shall see. Let's meet again tomorrow night, on my ship. That should give you enough time to come up with this 'plan' you mention, and then I shall decide how I feel about it. Deal?" He reached out his hand, and Jack, grinning, shook it.

"Deal!" he said.

"No deal!" Marcella shouted, but no one paid any attention to her.

"We are *doomed*," Teague muttered darkly from his chair.

But Jack wasn't worried. After all, overthrowing King Samuel wasn't exactly his real priority. All he needed was a plan that would distract Samuel long enough for Jack to get inside the fortress and grab the vial of Shadow Gold. He told himself he didn't particularly care what happened to Samuel or Libertalia afterwards. The Shadow Gold was the most important thing if Jack Sparrow was to survive to fight again another day.

Besides, he knew just who to ask for a crafty idea—Alex, the man who had sailed with the scheming Shadow Lord himself. Surely there was something in the Shadow Lord's bag of tricks that Jack could use against King Samuel.

Or if not . . . Jack just had to hope that his own brains were more than a match for any other Pirate Lord!

CHAPTER SEVEN

It was an odd group that assembled on Libertalia's dock two mornings later. The sun shone brightly in an azure blue sky, burning away the early morning clouds. On one side of the dock, the *Pearl* was swarming with activity as pirates and retired pirates climbed all over it, hammering and swabbing and putting everything to rights again. Once word got out that the captain, Jack Sparrow, might or might not be related to Libertalia's own lord, Captain

Teague, Billy had had no trouble finding skilled men who were eager to help fix up the ship. He told Jack they would be ready to sail again in just one day.

"Ah, we'll be back by then," Jack said, clapping his old friend on the shoulder. "I mean, how long can it take to walk across an island, sneak into a king's fort, steal a vial, and overthrow him? Right? Right."

Billy looked glumly dubious, but he didn't argue. He was willing to stay with the ship waiting for Jack, but if word came back that Samuel had defeated him, Billy was also more than willing to take the *Pearl* and sail on back to North Carolina without him. He missed his wife and son, whom Jack had promised to return him to months ago. At this point, he knew he had no choice but to sail on . . . he just had to hope he'd get home again at the end of Jack's latest wild adventure.

"You know, *I* could stay with the ship instead of Billy," Barbossa offered slyly. "He'd be a great asset to you in this battle, and you can certainly trust me with the *Pearl.* . . ."

"Nonsense!" Jack cried, and Barbossa frowned, worried for a moment that Jack knew how untrustworthy Barbossa really was. But then Jack went on: "You're a great asset, too, Hector. I mean, not amazing or anything, but don't sell yourself short; I bet you can take out at *least* one pirate with that pistol of yours. Or scare 'em off with your face! Ha! And away we go!" He swung down to the dock on a long rope, missing the ferocious glare Barbossa sent after him.

Barbossa's nose this morning was enormous and purple as a result of the battle in the dark. He'd covered it with a hideous bandage, but it gave him an even more menacing look than usual. Not to mention that he could not seem to get the smell of cod out of his hair. The first mate fumed. He knew exactly which pirate he wanted to take out with his pistol . . . as soon as he had a chance.

Carolina was already on the dock, stretching. She felt tense and uncomfortable from two nights of sleeping on a regular bed again. Teague was a hospitable host, and his food was much better than what they got on the *Pearl*, but Carolina had a hard time sleeping without the creak of the hammocks and the swaying of the boat. She longed to be back at sea again as soon as possible.

The only upside to being on land was that it was easier to get away from Diego and Marcella. Whenever Diego came looking for her, she could escape into the jungle around Teague's mansion and just walk for hours. Madagascar was full of strange animals and plants she'd never seen before; it was also one of the most beautiful places she'd ever been. She could see why the pirates had chosen it for their secret utopian hideout.

Marcella sashayed past, batting her eyelashes at herself in that silver mirror again. Carolina was so sick of that mirror. She wished she could grab it and throw it into the bay. But then Marcella would pitch a fit and Carolina would have to hear about it for the rest of the voyage, so it wasn't worth it.

On the other side of the dock, an old, practically rotting ship bobbed alongside the gleaming *Ranger*, Jocard's vessel. This was a key part of Jack's clever plan (*extremely* clever, if he did say so himself, even if it was based on tales Alex had told him of the Shadow Lord's methods). Jocard's first mate, Marcus, would sail around the island on the *Ranger*, towing the old ship behind him. Then the *Ranger* would hide, and a skeleton crew of a few brave men—the best swimmers on Jocard's crew—would sail the old ship at Samuel's fortress as if they were attacking it. This decoy would draw the attention of the fort's defenders . . . while the real threat snuck up on them from an entirely different direction.

Jocard shook his head, looking over the ragtag bunch of pirates who followed Jack. He squinted particularly suspiciously at Catastrophe Shane, who had already tripped over his boots and nearly fallen into the bay four times.

"This will never work," Jocard rumbled. "Real pirates don't attack from land. No one's ever tried to get to Samuel's fort through the jungle before—and that's for a reason. It's impossible!"

"Precisely why he won't be expecting it," Jack said jauntily. "Nothing's impossible, Jocard! Except getting Grandmama to shut up, of course. Thank heaven we're finally getting away from her!"

"Ahahaha!" Jack jumped as the old lady's cackle echoed over the bay. Grandmama stumped onto the dock with her cane, dressed in the strangest old-fashioned pirate outfit any of them had ever seen. An oversize lime green frock coat came down to her knees. A bright purple bandanna peeked out from under a floppy black hat. Dark blue pants were bunched up and wrinkled over black leather boots. Her long white shirt was bursting with lacy frills, and the small ruby gleamed from her false teeth.

"Getting away from me, eh?" she crowed, poking Jack's stomach with the end of her cane. "Is that what you think? Not on your life, sonny boy! I'm comin' with you, I am! You need a real pirate on this mission, you do!"

"Oh, yes?" Jack said. "You mean you? Someone who's just as likely to stab me in the back as any of the folks we're fighting?"

"Exactly," Grandmama said. "A real pirate!"

"No." Jack groaned. "You can't come with us! We'll be hiking through miles of jungle! It's no trip for a—er, for a—" The baleful glare on Grandmama's face warned him off finishing that sentence. "For an exceptionally fit and attractive old pirate?" he tried instead.

A clatter of boots sounded on the *Ranger*'s gangplank, and they turned to see a strikingly tall woman striding toward them. Her bronze skin glowed and her long, dark hair was thick and lustrous as Carolina's. She beamed at Jocard with perfect white teeth.

"Ah, Sarah," Jocard said. "Jack, I want you to meet my betrothed. Sarah is going to lead us through the jungle, as she grew up around these parts and knows the area well. She comes from a wealthy Portuguese family—it will be a fortunate alliance for me indeed." He put his arm around Sarah and she tipped her hat to Jack's crew with a superior smile.

"Betrothed!" Marcella gasped from behind Carolina. "Her! Betrothed! To you!" She shook her head, recovering from the shock. "What, someone actually agreed to marry *you*?" she sniped at Jocard. Before he could answer, she hurried on. "Well, that's just fine! Nobody even cares! I don't know why you're even telling us, because it's not like anyone wants to know! You'll make a stupid husband anyway!"

Carolina stared at Marcella in surprise, and Sarah obviously was about to make a cutting retort, when Grandmama suddenly threw off her coat, let out a bloodcurdling scream, hurtled across the dock, and tackled Sarah.

Everyone yelled in alarm as the two women plummeted over the side and into the water. An enormous splash soaked all the pirates on the dock.

"Sarah!" Jocard shouted. "Quick! Somebody help her!"

"Grandmama!" Jack shouted. "Quick! Somebody drown her!"

It was hard to see what was happening with all the splashing and shrieking coming from the bay, but it looked like Grandmama was trying to drag Sarah under and tear out her hair at the same time.

Sarah was fighting back furiously, knocking the old lady's hat off and struggling to get away. She managed to lunge toward the dock, but then Grandmama caught her arm and sank her teeth into Sarah's wrist.

"OW!" Sarah howled, lashing out with her legs. She kicked Grandmama square in the stomach and knocked her loose, but before she could grab Jocard's outstretched hand, Grandmama wrapped her bony arms around Sarah's waist, heaved in a deep breath, and dragged her below the surface of the water.

"What is the meaning of this?" Jocard roared,

throwing off his coat and boots. But a few others were ahead of him: splash after splash sounded as Diego, Marcus, and Carolina all dove into the water to intervene.

It was a ferocious (and very wet) battle, but finally Carolina and Diego were able to haul Grandmama away from Sarah long enough for Marcus to heave Jocard's fiancée back onto the dock. Sarah stood next to Jocard, dripping and panting with exhaustion, and they both glared down at Grandmama, who was still kicking and flailing in the water even though Carolina and Diego had a firm grip on each of her arms.

"You're a madwoman!" Sarah yelled. Her voice was rich and deep with a Portuguese accent. "Why would you attack a total stranger? What is wrong with you?"

"HAH!" Grandmama shouted, then sputtered as a wave of water swamped over her head. "I know you! I never forget a face, Teresa!

You think you can sneak past me! Hah!"

Sarah looked utterly baffled. "I have no idea who this 'Teresa' is," she said to Jocard, pulling her long wet hair back and wringing it out. "This old woman must be senile."

"I'll show you senile!" Grandmama howled, nearly punching Diego in the nose as she waved her fists around. "I remember the day we met! It was right after you gave birth to that blackguard Samuel! I saw what a wretched little monster he'd be—I saw it in his eyes the minute he was born! And having a mother like you didn't help!"

The pirates on the dock exchanged puzzled and amused glances.

"Um, Grandmama," Jack said politely, "far be it from me to contradict you . . . but this Samuel fellow is at least thirty-five years old. There's no way our new friend Sarah here could be his mother."

"What?" Grandmama stopped splashing for a moment and took a long look at Sarah.

The Portuguese woman tossed her head. "All right, yes. My family is distantly related to the mother of this 'King Samuel.' But she was thrown out of the family long ago and died while Samuel was young. I have never met her, and none of my relatives ever speak of her."

"It's true," Jocard said with a nod. "Sarah told me all this already. She has spent time in Samuel's fort—which is what makes her the perfect guide for our invasion."

"Oh," Grandmama said. "I see. Very well, then." She wrenched her arms out of Carolina and Diego's grasps and adjusted her bandanna. In a moment she had climbed back onto the dock with her strong, wrinkled arms and was standing in a puddle of water, glaring defiantly around at everyone. "Well?" she snapped. "Don't we have a fortress to attack? Come on, you lazy layabouts!" She snatched her coat from where she'd dropped it and marched off toward the jungle, head held high.

"Well," Jean said, helping Carolina and Diego up as the other pirates hurried after Grandmama, "that was certainly exciting."

"Every day with Grandmama is a new adventure," Jack said with a toothy grin. "Just don't ever touch her cane, or you'll end up much better acquainted with it than you would like. Consider yourselves warned." He made an ominous, wide-eyed face, and then galloped after the others.

Carolina noticed that Marcella had gone ahead with the pirates instead of waiting for Diego, even though she had insisted on coming along because she "couldn't be parted for a minute from my dear Diego!" She looked down at her wet friend with a thoughtful expression.

Diego shook his head and sighed. "I just

hope the rest of the mission is nowhere near as 'exciting' as this!"

"Oh, sure," Jean said. "What are the chances of that?"

Not far away, across a stretch of sparkling blue ocean, the pale figure of Benedict Huntington strode across the deck of the *Peacock*, tapping a long hunting crop against his white trousers. One sailor didn't scurry out of his way fast enough, and Benedict struck him across the face with the crop, sending the man away howling.

"McTavish!" Benedict shouted. His first mate, a wiry man covered in freckles from head to toe, came running from the wheel and saluted. Roland McTavish was smart and capable and a good navigator, but most important, he was an excellent toady. He knew better than anyone how to say "Yes, sir!" and "Absolutely, sir!" and "What a marvelous idea, sir!" to

Captain Huntington, which was how he had lasted so long in his position.

"Yes, sir!" he barked.

"Make sail for the fort of King Samuel," Benedict said, handing Roland a rolled-up chart. "It's on the western coast of Madagascar."

"Aye-aye, sir!" McTavish said with another salute. "May I ask a question, sir?"

Benedict's cold, pale blue eyes bored into his. "Only if it doesn't annoy me."

McTavish gulped. "Just wondering, sir—why it is we're not going to Libertalia anymore?"

With a smirk on his face, Benedict patted his vest pocket. "Let's just say I have inside information about where the pirates will be next—and it's King Samuel's fort. Understand?"

"Absolutely, sir!" McTavish saw Benedict's wife coming and hurriedly backed away. Barbara scared him even more than Benedict; he had frequent nightmares in which she decided to slit the throats of the entire crew on a whim. The horrible thing was, he believed she could easily do it in real life.

"So," Barbara said, watching Roland trot off, "what are you going to tell Samuel when we get there?"

"That I have lucrative business ideas to discuss with him about our mutual interests in the trade routes around the Indian Ocean," Benedict said smoothly.

Barbara's perfect eyebrows went up. "You're not going to tell him about the attack coming from inland?"

His smile made him look like an albino cobra planning his next meal. "And miss the opportunity to watch pirates tear each other apart? By no means. Nor do I want to explain where my information is coming from. But most of all, I want Jack Sparrow to get inside the fort."

"You do?" Barbara said, surprised. "But what

about the letter from the Shadow Lord? Didn't he specifically ask you to keep the two Pirate Lords apart?"

"Ah, don't you worry about that. Jack Sparrow will be dead long before he reaches King Samuel." Benedict licked his lips hungrily. "I want to be there waiting for him." His voice dropped to a chilling growl. "I want to kill him myself."

"Oooooh," Barbara said, her green eyes glittering. "You're right . . . that does sound like a lot more fun."

CHAPTER EIGHT

Who knew, Jack Sparrow thought to himself as he traipsed through the sweltering jungle of Madagascar, that there were quite so many insects in the world? He slapped away another mosquito and jumped to avoid a large flying beetle of some sort. As he flailed his hands, he accidentally whapped Barbossa's hat and nearly knocked it off his head. Barbossa turned to scowl horribly at him over his bandage, and Jack reacted with exaggerated horror.

"Oh, sorry, Hector," he said. "I forgot about the old nose there—didn't recognize you for a minute. Thought perhaps ghouls were rising out of the ground to attack us."

"I don't sense any dead bodies underfoot," Alex said gravely, shuffling through the underbrush behind Jack. "Doubtful that ghouls could rise here, Captain Jack Sparrow."

"I didn't know zombies could sense corpses," Carolina said, regarding him with curiosity.

"Ew," Marcella said. "You're all so GROSS! Stop talking about corpses RIGHT NOW." She elbowed her way forward until she was right behind Sarah and Jocard, who were leading the way through the jungle. They'd been walking for half a day already, stopping only for water. Sarah moved quickly and silently, as did Jocard and his men. Jack's crew . . . not so much.

Catastrophe Shane tripped over another tree

root and let out a howl of agony as he crashed to the jungle floor.

"Shhh!" Sarah hissed, whipping around with a finger to her lips. "You never know if King Samuel might have decided to post guards on this side. We have to be very careful!"

"Why'd you let him come, anyway?" Diego asked Jack as he helped Shane to his feet.

"He was complaining that he never got to go on any of the missions," Jack said with a shrug. "Besides, he offered to carry my luggage." He waved at the large sack Shane was hauling over one shoulder.

"Luggage? On a battle mission?" Barbossa snorted. "Typical."

"You never know when you might get hungry," Jack pointed out. "Oooh, look, a banana!" He pulled a long yellow fruit off a nearby tree and started peeling it. Jean's eyes nearly popped out of his head.

"Jean's stomach growled loudly. "Wow. I'm going to find something to eat, too!" He looked around at the trees as they began walking again and rubbed his empty stomach.

While they were talking, Carolina was watching Marcella. Jean's cousin had been stealthily busy while the other pirates stood still, glaring at Catastrophe Shane. She had drawn a long loop of vine out of her skirt—obviously something she'd been hiding for a while. She had carefully tossed it right in front of Sarah's feet . . . so that once they started walking again, Sarah stepped right into it. The loop closed over her ankle, and she tripped and fell with a huge thud.

"SHHHHHHHHHHHHHH!" Marcella scolded her loudly. "*Jeez*, Sarah, how ungraceful are *you*? Plus, like, totally a hypocrite! You're the loudest one of all! Right? Am I right?" She glanced sideways at Jocard, but he was hurrying to Sarah's side and didn't seem to notice Marcella's tirade.

"Are you all right?" he asked Sarah.

"I'm fine," she said, glaring daggers at Marcella. Her eyes softened as she looked up at Jocard. "But perhaps I should rest this ankle for a moment. Would you mind carrying me, darling?"

"Not at all," Jocard said, scooping her up in his strong arms.

It was hard to miss the triumphant expression Sarah shot at Marcella over Jocard's shoulder. Carolina twisted her hair around one finger thoughtfully as Marcella stomped to the back of the group again, obviously fuming.

"Heh-heh-heh," Grandmama cackled, thwacking branches aside with her cane. "Pirate men never change, do they? Oblivious as always!" She gave Carolina a wicked look. "Of course, some pirate women aren't very observant, either."

Carolina blushed. She could guess what

Grandmama was talking about—Diego hadn't taken his eyes off her all day. It was much easier to notice now that Marcella wasn't throwing herself on him nonstop. Apparently, she had chosen someone else to torment, for her own mysterious Marcella reasons.

"Hey, Jean," Carolina said, avoiding Grandmama's eyes. The curly-headed pirate had come back from a bush stuffing something in his mouth. "What did you find to eat?"

"I dunno," he said, holding out a handful of purple berries. "But they're delici—*urk*!" He grabbed his throat, choking.

"Jean!" Carolina cried. She thumped him on the back. "Jean, are you okay?"

"Jean!" Marcella shrieked, grabbing him around the waist. His choking noises got worse.

Sarah dropped out of Jocard's arms and came running back to them. "What is it?" she asked. "What did he eat?"

Carolina showed her the berries, and Sarah frowned worriedly.

"Oh, no!" Marcella wailed. "He's going to die! I'm going to be left all alone with horrible pirates in a horrible, smelly jungle!"

"He's not going to die," Sarah snapped. "But these berries do have . . . unusual side effects."

Jean suddenly lunged upright and froze, his hands outstretched in front of him. Carolina gasped as she saw his face. His eyes were rolled back in his head so only the whites were showing. All the color had drained from his cheeks, making his freckles stand out like dark spots of blood on snow.

"The Day of the Shadow is coming," he murmured in a spooky voice that sounded nothing like his normal, cheerful one.

A shiver ran down Jack's spine. "Come again?" he said, hoping he'd heard wrong.

"The Day of the Shadow . . . it draws closer

and closer . . ." Jean said softly. "The Day of the Shadow will be here soon."

"What is he talking about?" Marcella asked, her eyes wide and frightened. "Jean, stop it! Stop teasing! Act normal!"

"He can't help it," Sarah said. "These berries give people visions of the future." She crushed them in her fist and dropped them on the ground. "He was foolish to eat them. Leave him here or carry him with us—he'll be like this for hours."

She spun and strode ahead through the trees. Carolina noticed that her ankle seemed to be just fine. "And hurry!" Sarah called over her shoulder. "We must be ready to attack King Samuel's fort at dawn, when the decoy ship is launched!"

"Hustle bustle, hurry flurry," Jack muttered.

"Your cousin will be all right," Jocard said kindly, patting Marcella's shoulder. "Don't worry, Marcella."

"Like you know anything!" Marcella retorted, but he was already turning away to catch up with Sarah.

"Visions of the future?" Jack echoed. "Well, that doesn't sound so bad. Hey, Jean lad, tell me—how soon will I make my first million doubloons? Or, I know—have my pretty lass friends back in Tortuga forgotten about me yet? Or how about this—where can I find the best rum, eh?"

"He's not a crystal ball," Marcella snapped as Diego and Alex awkwardly draped Jean's arms over their shoulders and dragged him forward.

"Betrayal," Jean whispered, turning his unseeing eyes toward Jack. "Betrayal awaits you. . . ."

"Uh-oh," Jack said, looking alarmed. "Not good."

"I see an island," Jean went on. "You're alone on an island with buried rum, lots of rum. . . ."

Jack's face lit up. "Much better!" he declared. "Not bad at all! Er—how much rum, exactly?"

"The Day of the Shadow is coming," Jean said again, and his head lolled to the side. Diego staggered as Jean's weight sagged against his shoulder.

"He's talking about the Shadow Lord," Carolina said to Jack. "He must be! The Day of the Shadow—do you know what that means?"

"Trifles," Jack said, waving her off. "Probably nothing to worry about. Mad ravings. Every day has shadows in it, doesn't it? Bit of mumbo-jumbo, wobbly-babbly, that's all."

"Visions of the future, you mean," Carolina said. She hopped over a fallen tree trunk and hurried to keep up with Jack. Long strands of moss hung down in their faces and blue butter-flies darted away into the foliage. "Aren't you worried?"

"About being betrayed?" Jack said. "Piffle.

Who would betray someone as charming as me?"

It was lucky for Barbossa that Jack couldn't see the expression on his face at that moment.

"Don't do it!" Jean cried suddenly. His head popped up, and he nearly fell before Diego and Alex caught him. "Don't do it, Jack! Don't drink the last vial!"

Jack sprinted back, clearing the tree trunk in a single bound, and clapped a hand over Jean's mouth. He grinned wanly at Barbossa.

"What is he on about?" Barbossa growled. "Drinking the vials of Shadow Gold? Who would do that?"

"Good point, Hector," Jack said, nodding vigorously. "No one would do that! Pretty, shiny Shadow Gold! Drink it—that's crazy talk."

None of his crew members knew the truth: that Jack had to drink the Shadow Gold to cure his shadow-sickness. The rest of the pirates, including Barbossa, thought Jack was saving the Shadow Gold to sell at the end of their voyage, which would make them all fabulously wealthy. This seemed like a much better strategy to Jack than explaining to all of them that this whole trip was just to save his life. He was pretty sure they'd understand once he explained it to them at the end . . . or, failing that, he was pretty sure he could outrun them all.

Jean fought free of Jack's hand. "She'll die!" he gasped hoarsely. "If you take the last vial . . . I see it—she dies. I see her hair, long and dark— and the blood—so much blood. . . . She dies trying to save you, Jack! On the Day of the Shadow!"

Diego gasped. "He's talking about Carolina!" He grabbed Jack's shoulder and shook it. "He's saying Carolina is going to die!"

Carolina was speechless. Was it true? Was she destined to die fighting the Shadow Lord?

"Well, you know how these prophecy thingies are," Jack said, trying not to look worried. "All vague and cryptic and, uh . . . cryptic and vague."

"Ooooh, not all of them," Grandmama chirped. Her black eyes sparked with malevolent glee at the anxious looks on all their faces. "Some prophecies are spot-on. Like the one Cousin Mabeltrude the Violent Visionary had about you nearly burning down my ship when you were eight. Lucky she predicted it, too, or we mightn't have had the foresight to lock you in the brig where you couldn't do too much damage."

"That wasn't a vision," Jack insisted balefully. "All eight-year-old boys like fire. *Anyone* could have guessed that."

"Skeletons in the moonlight!" Jean shrieked. "They look alive, but they're not! Cursed, they're all cursed! Even the monkey!" Suddenly he slumped again, losing consciousness against Diego's shoulder.

"See?" Jack said triumphantly. "Utter non-sense!"

"Huh. That did sound pretty ridiculous," Diego admitted.

"Come on, let's catch up to the others," Jack said. They started forward again, dragging Jean carefully along with them.

"Jack . . . watch out . . . he's out there waiting . . ." Jean murmured.

"The Shadow Lord?" Jack said quietly.

"And the other one . . . thirteen years, Jack . . . and then he sends his pet. Beware, for the beastie brings your death. . . ."

Diego looked at Jack quizzically.

"More nonsense!" Jack said. "Ha-ha! Rambling! Makes no sense to anybody! Especially not to me! No, sir!" He patted his forehead with his kerchief and edged away from

Jean, stumbling over fallen branches.

Unfortunately, he knew exactly what that last comment was about, and who the dark character was that was waiting for him out in the world. And since nobody else knew about that . . . Jack had to wonder whether that meant Jean's other words were going to come true as well.

CHAPTER NINE

The imposing stone fort of King Samuel, Pirate Lord of the Atlantic Ocean, sat on a high cliff overlooking a bay, with views all the way to the ocean. Guards patrolled the ramparts day and night, keeping a sharp eye out for approaching ships.

But they had never seen anything quite like the ship that was slowly limping into the bay at that moment. Pale gold and pink streaked the dawn sky with only a few thin clouds overhead, and because of the bluff the fort was built on, the sun was angled to rise almost directly behind the ship. Its drab, dirty sails were barely fluttering in the early morning breeze. The guards couldn't see any movement on the deck—it almost looked like a ghost ship sailing forth without a crew.

One thing it did have, though: cannons. Gun and cannon barrels poked out of every hole. The ship might not have looked like a threat otherwise, but the guards knew King Samuel would want to hear about those cannons.

"Go sound the alarm," said the head guard, squinting against the sun. "We'll treat it as an attack."

"A rather pathetic attack," snorted one of the other guards.

"Hey," said a third, "is that . . . *smoke* coming out of the portholes?"

They all fell silent. Their eyes were dazzled by

the rising sun, and it was hard to see. It did seem as if thin dark smoke were trickling from a few of the ship's portholes.

"They're lighting their cannons already!" said the head guard. "Quick, get everyone to the ships! We must shoot it out of the water before it has a chance to shoot us!"

Pandemonium erupted in the fort. Pirates ran in all directions, gathering their weapons. King Samuel strode out onto the highest rampart to see this mysterious ship for himself. His bald head gleamed like ebony in the sunlight, which sparkled off his large gold earrings. He swept his leopard-skin robe around him and lifted his chin regally.

"It could be a trick," his deep voice boomed. "Like a Trojan horse—anything could be inside. Approach with caution—do not get close enough to be boarded! Just shoot at the ship from afar!"

He turned to his guests and smiled an insincerely toothy smile. "Nothing to worry about, my European friends. Foolish pirates often try to prove their strength by attacking King Samuel. And then they prove their mortality—by dying."

"Mm-hmm," Benedict said noncommittally, shooting his wife a significant look. Barbara fluttered her *Peacock* fan in front of her face and sidled closer to King Samuel.

"You must be very brave," she said with a coy expression. "Getting attacked all the time! I can't even imagine. When was the last time—and what did you do?"

King Samuel loved to talk about himself (often in the third person), as Benedict and Barbara had learned painfully over dinner the night before. He loved showing off for visitors from all parts of the world, impressing them with tales of his manliness and strength, his cunning and power. The Huntingtons had suffered through an endless walk through Samuel's trophy room, where he kept the heads of animals he'd killed and treasures from ships he'd sunk or pirates he'd robbed.

Samuel's favorite pastime—apart from betraying fellow pirates for large piles of gold—was hunting and trapping wild animals in Africa, then bringing them back alive on his ship. As a result, the fort was inhabited by a strange wandering menagerie. Barbara had not been pleased when an enormous tiger sauntered through her bedroom in the middle of the night, nor was she particularly fond of the parrots that fluttered through the rafters while they ate dinner. And she was fairly certain that a ridiculously tall spotted creature with a neck as long as a tree had poked its head in her window while she was dressing that morning. If you asked her, it was downright unsanitary.

Now Samuel launched into an endless story about a wayward Arabic ship that had run into a storm and made the terrible mistake of seeking shelter in his bay. Riveted by Barbara's hypnotic green eyes, he didn't notice Benedict slinking away in search of the landward entrance to Samuel's fort.

For indeed there was one—a small wooden door in a large stone wall. Samuel's men used it to get to the jungle when they needed food or building supplies. It was locked, but no one bothered to guard it. What self-respecting pirate would ever attack by land instead of by sea? Not only that, but the terrain for miles around was a tangle of forest and marsh where nobody would want to live, or even travel.

And yet . . . emerging from the trees at that very moment were the latest pirates to attempt an attack on King Samuel's fort. Sarah led them up to the door, and they stood around it for a moment, catching their breath.

They had spent a very unpleasant night in the rain forest, sleeping in mud and swarmed by mosquitoes. It also didn't help that Jean kept sitting up suddenly with howls of: "The Day of the Shadow is coming!" or "Don't take the gold! It's cursed!" or "She's going to die!" or "The monkey's name is Jack!" (This last one caused Barbossa endless amusement, and he filed it away in his memory for future use.)

Fortunately, when they finally arose to travel on a few hours before dawn, Jean had recovered. He was still woozy and pale, but his eyes were back to normal, and he couldn't remember a thing about his visions. When Jack tried to ask him some pointed questions, Jean just blinked at him in confusion.

"That's all right, then," Jack had said brightly. "Let's all just forget it ever happened." But the coming "Day of the Shadow" threat hung over them all, and for a couple of people in particular, the words that seemed to hint at Carolina's death were even more terrifying. Jack wanted to forget it more than anyone. If Jean was right, then drinking the last vial of Shadow Gold would mean Carolina's death. But *not* drinking it meant Jack would die—Tia Dalma had told him specifically that he needed all seven to be cured. So what was he going to do?

"This is the door?" Jack said, shoving those thoughts aside. "Doesn't look like much."

"Oh, and I'm sure *your* fort has the best defenses in the world," Sarah snapped. She was in a particularly bad mood this morning. Someone had dropped bitter tree bark into her soup the night before and then filled her hair with beetles while she was sleeping. Of course, almost everyone could guess exactly who that *someone* was, but Marcella protested innocence when Jean asked her about it, and Grandmama fended off any other interrogators by thumping them with her cane.

The ancient pirate seemed to have taken a liking to Marcella, which didn't surprise Jack at all. Naturally the two most irritating women he'd ever met would hit it off. They were probably plotting some new way to annoy him at this very moment.

He narrowed his eyes at them, but Grandmama's attention was fixed on the door. Her eyes were shining, and her sword was already out of its sheath. She was the only one who'd gotten a good night's rest, and she was raring to leap into battle.

Even from the outside, the pirates could hear shouting and crashes inside the fort.

"The distraction is working," Jocard said in a low, calm voice. "We must go now."

"The door will be locked," Sarah said. "We'll have to hack through the wood. I know a few of you brought axes; the rest can use their swords."

"Hang on," Jack said. "Before we blunt our lovely steel on this impediment to our progress, how about we at least *try* the doorknob?" He sidled around Sarah, who put her hands on her hips and huffed impatiently.

"Do what you like, but there's no point!" she said. "I've been here before; I know this door is always locked. . . ." Her voice trailed off as the door swung smoothly open under Jack's hand.

"Funny," Jack said. "Always locked, eh? All evidence to the contrary?"

"Oh, shut up," Sarah said, shoving him aside and storming through the door.

"I was going to *say* ladies first," Jack called after her.

The other pirates bundled through the door en masse, drawing daggers, swords, and pistols in a swarm of red kerchiefs and rotten-toothed grins. Just inside the door was a small round vestibule and a long hallway leading to a set of stone stairs and two doors. Jack guessed that at least one of the doors probably led into the kitchen, which could often be found on this level in forts like this. For one thing, it made it easier to drag dead carcasses straight from the hunt to the cooks for cleaning and roasting.

"Don't forget!" Jocard called above the fray. "King Samuel is mine!"

Jack bowed pleasantly as everyone tumbled past him. He was perfectly happy to let other people be the first ones into battle. Cleaning up afterward was more his line of work. Picking up any treasure that got accidentally dropped along the way, for example.

He nipped inside after the last pirate had entered and turned to close the door behind him. The footsteps of his crew's boots were pounding away down the hall as the door clicked shut.

Suddenly he felt cold steel pressing into his neck, and he froze.

"I've been waiting for you, Jack Sparrow," said the voice of Benedict Huntington.

CHAPTER TEN

"**W**aiting for me?" Jack said, looking down at the sword pointed nastily at his neck. "That's terribly thoughtful, but you didn't have to do that, mate." He tried to take a step back in the cramped space, but Benedict pressed the sword more forcefully into his skin and Jack winced. He could feel a trickle of blood sliding down his shoulder. How very inconvenient. Bloodstains were horribly difficult to get out of shirts.

"I'm not your *mate*," Benedict snarled. "I am your death."

"Ah, but see, that's where you're wrong," Jack said blithely. "Bad news, I'm afraid. I have it on good authority that the pet beastie is the one who's going to kill me. So I'm afraid that if *it's* going to kill me, then *you* can't. Savvy?"

"Stop blithering," Benedict said. "I'm going to read you a list of your crimes before I execute you." He fished a scroll out of his coat pocket with his free hand and unrolled it dramatically.

Jack looked pained. "Oh, dear. Couldn't you please just kill me instead?"

"For the crime of piracy on the high seas; humiliating a superior officer of the East India Trading Company—"

"Aw, did I hurt your feelings?" Jack said. "I hear that a lot— Good God, what is *that*?" He stared off over Benedict's shoulder with an astonished, horrified expression.

Benedict snorted. "As if I would ever fall for a stupid trick like that."

Jack's horrified expression didn't change.

"Sparrow, stop being a simpleton. I'm not a fool, you know."

Jack relaxed his face and shrugged. "Well, it was worth a try."

"Idiot," Benedict growled, glancing back down at his list. "Destruction of royal propertyyyeeeeeeEEEEAAUUUUUGH!" Benedict's chilly recitation turned into a high-pitched shriek as something lifted him off his feet and threw him down the narrow stone hall-way.

"Told you!" Jack said smugly, then he dodged as the "something" turned and came for him.

It looked like some kind of man-beast with black fur and enormous, bulging arms. Its nose was large and flat and its brow hung heavily over its eyes. At first Jack had barely noticed it in the shadowy corner of the vestibule; he'd assumed it was a stuffed hunting prize or a statue. That was until it moved.

Now it was moving again, and moving *fast*, with a rolling gait powered by its front knuckles. Jack sped off down the hall, his arms flapping wildly as he ran. He leaped gracefully over Benedict, who was still scrambling backward with terror written all over his face.

"ARRRRR!" roared the beast, charging after Jack. There wasn't time to get up the stairs so he whipped open the nearest door. As he'd expected: a kitchen, enormous and empty of people. Unfortunately it had no other exits— but Jack was out of options. He turned to slam the door behind him and found Benedict blocking the gap.

"LET ME IN!" Benedict bellowed, trying to squeeze in as Jack tried to shove him back out again. "DON'T LET IT EAT ME!"

They struggled back and forth for a moment, but the pale man's desperation won out. Benedict squished his skeletal frame through the gap and stumbled onto the stone flagstones of the kitchen floor.

Jack grabbed a chair and shoved it against the door handle just as a ferocious pounding started on the other side of the door. He jumped back and saw splinters of wood already flying loose.

"Help me!" Jack shouted, seizing a small wooden table. Benedict scrambled over to grab the other end and together they braced it against the door.

"That ought to hold the beast for a moment," Jack said, turning with a pleased expression—which immediately dropped off his face as he saw Benedict drawing a second sword. His first was lying on the stones in the vestibule, but evidently this was a man who came prepared. His second sword was a whip-thin rapier, and it was already in motion toward Jack's neck.

"Just long enough for me to kill you," Benedict snarled, but this time Jack had time to dodge out of reach. He drew his own sword and danced around the long, heavy table in the center of the room. Benedict followed with measured steps, his reptilian eyes focused unblinkingly on Jack.

"Downright unsporting, that is," Jack said in an injured voice. "I just saved your life."

"You tried to push me back into the hall!" Benedict shouted.

"Well, but I didn't succeed, did I?" Jack protested.

BOOM! BOOM! BOOM! went the beast's fists against the door.

Quick as lightning, Benedict lunged forward with his rapier, but Jack leaped to the side just in time. He hurled himself over the table, seized a copper pot, and threw it at Benedict's head. It was rather a Grandmama-like move, but Jack couldn't be choosy at this stage—and besides, Grandmama had won every fight she'd ever been in, so her methods were clearly nothing to sneeze at.

The pot glanced off Benedict's shoulder and he grunted angrily. Instead of diving over it as Jack had, Benedict ran up onto the table and jumped off, kicking out at Jack as he fell. The side of his boot connected with Jack's ribs, and Jack nearly dropped his sword. Benedict hit the ground and spun upright again, just in time to get a pot lid in the face. He staggered back as Jack darted to the far end of the table.

Panting with rage, Benedict chased him. A few strands of pale blond hair were sticking up from his usually smooth head and a small trickle of blood ran from his nose, but he didn't seem to notice. His eyes flared with hatred.

Jack started grabbing everything within reach

and throwing it. Spoons, dishes, and cooking tongs flew through the air, most of them clattering harmlessly around Benedict as he whacked them aside with his sword. At the last second, Jack brought up his own sword and met Benedict's with a resounding clang. Benedict pressed forward mercilessly, beating at Jack, but Jack had been studying his swordmanship for years—ever since losing a duel to an upstart, snobbish, untrustworthy aristocrat named Fitzwilliam, which forced him to let the traitor onboard his first ship, the *Barnacle*—a decision Jack had lived to regret.*

Now he was one of the best sword fighters in the Caribbean, and he matched Benedict's flashing blade strike for strike. They swung and pirouetted around the table, ducking under each other's blows, leaping over the low

*In *Jack Sparrow* Vol. 1: *The Coming Storm*

attacks. The light from the torches on the walls reflected off their swords as they parried and struck.

And all the while, the pounding at the door grew louder and louder. Jack glanced at it worriedly, noticing how a part of the wood was starting to cave into the room. It wouldn't be long before the creature broke through—and Jack didn't fancy fighting Benedict and a gigantic man-beast at the same time.

With a quick twist of his wrist, Jack flipped his sword under Benedict's and knocked the rapier out of the other man's hands. The thin sword flew across the kitchen and Benedict dove after it, which gave Jack enough time to leap onto the table and run all the way to the farthest end from the door. He hopped off and spun around just in time to see the door burst into pieces as the beast's fists punched through.

Roaring, the creature flung the small table out

of its way and lunged for Benedict, who was still getting to his feet with his sword.

Jack reacted by instinct. Much as he disliked the whole idea of Benedict, and especially the whole idea of Benedict "executing" Jack Sparrow, he still didn't want to see the man get his head munched off right in front of him.

He seized a huge platter, nearly as wide as the ship's wheel, from the nearest counter and threw it like a disk. It whizzed sideways through the air, fairly humming as it flew, and it struck the beast right in the shoulder.

The creature grunted in surprise, glanced sideways at Jack, and then turned right back to Benedict. It was as if it barely felt the plate hit. Benedict dropped his sword and backed away, gibbering with fear.

"Oi!" Jack hollered, dancing up and down and waving his arms. "Much tastier meat over here! Look at him, he's barely worth a mouthful!"

The beast reared up, lifted one massive paw, and backhanded Benedict across the face. Benedict staggered, his eyes rolling in his head, and then fell to the ground, unconscious. His arms splayed out to either side and his sword clattered to the flagstones. But Jack could see his chest still rising and falling, so Benedict wasn't dead yet.

"Oh, is that all you were going to do?" Jack said. "Have at it, then! Sorry to interrupt!"

But it was too late to hide now. The man-beast turned and started for Jack, lumbering purposefully across the kitchen. Its black fur rippled across its strong back and its long black feet gripped the stones as it charged.

Jack had escaped one enemy—but now he had to face an even bigger, scarier one.

CHAPTER ELEVEN

While Jack was battling Benedict and meeting his first gorilla in the fort kitchen, the other pirates were spreading out through King Samuel's fort. Jocard shouted orders, sending his men to capture and hold all the exits.

Jack's pirates were less disciplined, unsurprisingly. One of them heard a noise that sounded like sacks of gold clinking, and with a yell, most of them charged off to see what treasure they could find.

Carolina, Diego, and Jean, on the other hand, stayed close to Sarah and Jocard as they ran up flight after flight of stairs. Sarah seemed to know exactly where to go, and the others didn't question her. The distraction plan was working; they met little resistance, at least on the first few floors.

Carolina paused at a turn in one of the staircases and glanced out the window. She saw that most of Samuel's pirates had piled onto ships out in the bay. They had the smoking decoy ship surrounded and were firing madly into its side. They were probably only just starting to wonder why all those cannons weren't firing back.

And the answer was—those weren't cannons. The pirates of Libertalia had disguised the ship to look well-armed without wasting a single real gun. All of the cannon barrels sticking out of the ports were actually tree trunks and branches, painted to look like weaponry. The few pirates

Jocard had selected to steer the ship into the bay had set the ends of the branches that were inside on fire, making the ship look as if it were smoking. Then, once they saw Samuel's pirates pouring out of the fort to attack, Jocard's men dove into the water and swam back to the *Ranger*, which was waiting out of sight near some large rocks outside the bay.

The decoy ship sailed on, bobbing and weaving without anyone to steer it, and as the fire belowdecks spread and Samuel's cannon-balls began to smash into the sides, the entire ship burst into flames.

This only terrified Samuel's pirates more, as they didn't see anyone trying to put out the flames or dive to safety. All they saw was a fiery ghost ship, gliding relentlessly toward them. With shouts of terror, they kept blasting away at it—all the while missing the real attack going on *inside* the fort.

Carolina laughed. "It's working!" she cried, turning around and bumping into Diego. He grinned back at her.

"Some pirates are cleverer than others," he said. She gave him the first smile he'd seen from her in weeks, and then his heart jumped as she grabbed his hand.

"Come on—I want to meet this notorious King Samuel!" she said, tugging him up the stairs.

They caught up to the others at the next landing, where a trio of Samuel's pirates were waiting with their swords out.

"Intruders!" yelled the short, stocky one. "Warn the king!"

The tallest and skinniest of the three pirates turned to sprint away, but Jocard lunged past the outstretched swords and yanked him back by his long, matted hair. "Oh, no, you don't!" Jocard cried.

The other two turned to attack Jocard, but their swords clashed against Carolina's and Diego's swords instead. Carolina faced down the short one, who gave her a nasty glare. "She-pirates," he sneered. "I'd throw you all overboard if I could. Girls are bloody useless."

That was the wrong thing to say to Carolina. "You want to see useless?" she said, swinging her blade around. The short pirate barely got his sword up in time to stop hers from biting into his neck. He fell back with a shout, and she attacked again, driving him into the hallway behind him.

Diego's pirate was sickly-looking and blond, with several missing teeth, but he was stronger than Diego would have guessed. He immediately took advantage of his position and started to force Diego back down the stairs, unbalancing him with canny lunges and surprise twists of the blade.

Meanwhile, Jocard was rolling on the floor

with the tall, skinny pirate, exchanging bone-crunching kicks and punches to the face. "Sarah!" Jocard yelled. "Get me something to restrain him with!"

He glanced around, but in the melee of flying fists, he couldn't see Sarah anywhere. Suddenly Jean popped up beside him, grabbed one of the hanging tapestries from the wall, and yanked it down. A cloud of dust rose up, making all the pirates sneeze, and while the skinny one was doubled over coughing, Jocard flung the tapestry over his head and knocked him to the ground.

At the same time, Carolina kicked her opponent squarely in the middle of his chest. He flew backwards, landing with a thud on top of his defeated compatriot. Moments later, Diego was able to drive his pirate back up the stairs with a flurry of swordplay. The sickly blond pirate tripped over his fallen comrades and hit his head on the stone floor, knocking himself unconscious.

Jean found a long tasseled cord holding back a curtain in a nearby room, and they trussed the three pirates together in a heap. Jocard carefully covered them with the tapestry so they looked like a big pile of fabric instead of unconscious pirates.

"I hope that will give us more time," Jocard said. "I want the element of surprise when we reach King Samuel."

"Good idea," Sarah said, appearing at his elbow.

"Where did you go?" he asked.

"I checked the last flight of stairs ahead," she said. "It's all clear. He probably only has one or two guards left with him, since he has no reason to think he'll be attacked in his own throne room. This is the perfect chance to take him down! Come on!"

"Excellent thinking," he said, giving her a

one-armed hug. She tossed back her long dark hair and beckoned to the others.

Just then, they heard a pistol shot go off further down the stairs and whipped around, swords raised and ready to fight. But the bobbing blue plumes that came around the bend revealed that it was Barbossa on their heels, not another of Samuel's pirates. He had a new bruise forming on his forehead and splatters of blood on his left sleeve, but he was grinning with the excitement of battle.

"Now this is more like it!" he said.

"Where's Jack?" Jean asked, noticing for the first time that their captain wasn't with them. "And Marcella?"

Barbossa shrugged. He clearly couldn't care less about either of them.

"Who knows?" Diego said.

"That blond girl probably couldn't keep up." Sarah sniffed.

"And maybe Jack found someone else to fight," Carolina suggested, giving Barbossa a worried look.

"Huh," Barbossa growled. "Disappearing right when there's a real battle. Sounds like Jack." He spotted a pirate bearing down on them from a side hall and blasted his pistol into the man's leg.

"Quickly, or King Samuel will hear the commotion and get suspicious," Sarah said. They hurried on to the last flight of stairs, hearing the wounded pirate's howls of pain fade behind them.

"King Samuel's throne room is on the highest level," Sarah said as they ran. "That's where he always watches battles at sea."

"Doesn't sound very brave either," Carolina observed. "At least Jack is around somewhere, right?"

Barbossa snorted. "Probably drinking all the rum," he muttered.

150

* * *

Ironically, at that exact moment, Jack's hand *was* closing around a bottle of rum. Realizing what it was, he hesitated before throwing it.

"I just can't do it. Waste of good rum," he said, setting the bottle down again and grabbing the next nearest thing he could reach. Unfortunately, he'd already flung the thing through the air before he realized how useless it was.

The banana hit the man-beast square in the middle of its forehead, and it stopped in its tracks, blinking. Slowly it looked down at the fruit lying between its feet. With a low rumble, the man-beast lowered itself to its haunches, picked up the fruit, and began to eat it.

Jack gaped. It wasn't a man-eating beast after all! It was a gorilla—a hungry vegetarian—And it had probably smelled the other bananas in his coat, too. Maybe that was the whole reason it had come after them.

He started digging through his pockets. Now this was the kind of fight he liked!

The final staircase went around and around, up a stone tower into the sky, so even Jocard was getting winded toward the end. Sarah rounded the corner at the top and disappeared ahead of them. Jocard thundered after her, with Diego close on his heels.

Carolina was the next to reach the top of the stairs. And immediately she froze.

The throne room was a vast circular space decorated with treasures stolen from ships all over the Atlantic Ocean. Giant bronze vases stood on either side of the entrance from the stairs. Rich tapestries hung on the walls, and thick Oriental rugs covered the floor. Low, fur-covered seats edged the room under the windows, which looked out on the blue bay.

Spookiest of all, strange African animals

prowled in the corners and hung from the ceiling, so that the room was filled with muffled growls and hoots and squeaks. Carolina could see the glint of teeth in the shadows and hungry eyes watching from behind the throne.

But that wasn't what stopped her.

Nor was it the twelve armed guards, bristling with sharp weapons, all of them pointed at her and her friends.

No, what made Carolina freeze in her tracks was King Samuel, standing in the center of his throne room . . . holding a knife to Sarah's throat.

CHAPTER TWELVE

"No!" Jocard shouted. "Don't hurt her!" He took a step forward, and a wall of swords and spears clattered into place to stop him. Fuming, Jocard clenched his fists. "You won't get away with this," he growled at Samuel.

"Won't I?" Samuel said, caressing Sarah's cheek with the flat of his dagger blade. "Drop your sword, big man."

Jocard gritted his teeth.

"King Samuel orders you to drop it," Samuel

said harshly, pressing the knife into her neck. Sarah let out a small groan of pain.

"All right!" Jocard said. His sword hit the flagstones and a pair of guards snatched it away. Jocard held up his hands, palm out. "She is not your problem, Samuel. She's done nothing wrong. Let her go."

"Your friends, too," Samuel said, glaring at Diego, Carolina, Jean, and Barbossa, all lined up behind Jocard. "Disarm."

"I drop my sword for no man—or woman," Barbossa snarled.

"Would you like to watch her die?" Samuel asked Jocard, gripping Sarah's shoulder tightly.

"Do it," Jocard said to Barbossa in a low voice. "I am the captain here. I am telling you to drop your sword."

Barbossa's face twitched in a grimace of rage, but as the other three dropped their swords, he slowly bent over and placed his on the ground as well.

"Good," Samuel said with an insincere smile. "Now we can talk."

"First let her go," Jocard said. "She's not even a pirate. She's innocent in all this."

"Oh," Samuel said with a tsk-tsk-ing noise. "How sweet. And how wrong. Isn't that adorable, Sarah? He thinks you're innocent."

Sarah laughed as Samuel let her go. "Pirates always underestimate women," she said, winking at Jocard. She turned and sauntered down the length of the room, settling herself on the throne at the far end. She kicked one leg over the side and grinned at the surrounded pirates. "They don't do their research very well, either," she pointed out. "It's as if they had no idea at all that you have a half-sister, Samuel."

"You betrayed us," Jocard growled at her, fury darkening his face. "You were lying to me the whole time."

"State the obvious, why don't you?" Sarah

said with a yawn. "Oh, hello, Kitty. I missed you very much, yes I did." She leaned over and patted the sleek leopard that was rubbing its head against the side of the throne. It let out a rumbling purr, and Carolina and Diego both shuddered.

"You look familiar," Samuel said to Jocard, tapping his fingers together. He strolled forward and walked in a circle around the pirate captain, looking him up and down. "Does King Samuel know you from somewhere?"

"Of course you wouldn't remember," Jocard said. "You've stolen so many lives. One family—one young boy—that means nothing to you. It probably took but a minute of your time, and you haven't thought about them again since."

"Ah," Samuel said. "That explains this foolhardy attack. Revenge, is it? Listen, if I had to explain myself to every ignorant child I've sold into slavery, I'd never have time for anything else. That's the way the world works. I'm a pirate, you know. I'll take my money however I can get it."

"A true pirate still has some honor," Jocard said. "And a man who calls himself a king should have more care for his subjects."

Samuel paused in front of Jocard, raising his eyebrows. But before he could speak, Jocard spat in his face.

The guards in the room lunged forward as one, but Samuel raised his hand calmly to stop them.

"No, we're not going to kill him," Samuel announced, wiping his face with the corner of his leopard-skin robe. "There's obviously only one perfect punishment for this man—and that is to go back where he came from. I bet I can get a lot of money for you." He glanced over the pirates behind Jocard. "And you," he said, pointing to Diego. His gaze landed on Barbossa. "You, not so much."

Jocard started to chuckle. "You really think you've won," he said, shaking his head. "You have no idea."

Samuel turned to stare at him. "No idea about what?"

"No idea who else is in the fort with us." Jocard looked Samuel straight in the eye. "That's right. Captain Jack Sparrow."

"Just misunderstood, aren't you?" Jack said, handing the gorilla another banana. "Really quite a friendly, er . . . man-beast-ape-thingie, you are." He was sitting on the edge of the table, swinging his legs. On the floor beside him, the gorilla was contentedly munching on all the fruit Jack had been able to find.

Jack leaned over and prodded Benedict's prone body with the tip of his sword. He widened his kohl-lined eyes when Benedict still didn't move.

"Nope," he said to the gorilla. "Still out. Good punch you've got on you there." He tipped back his hat. "Well, I can't leave until he wakes up to hear my dramatic exit line. I've been working on it for weeks. You want to hear it?"

"AAOURRAAGRRAARRRGH," said the gorilla, snatching another banana from Jack's hand.

"Maybe later then," Jack said pleasantly. "No hurry."

"Well, if he's going to rescue us, I hope he hurries up and does it soon," Jean muttered as Samuel's pirates started binding their wrists.

CRASH!

All the pirates in the throne room jumped.

"What was that?" Samuel demanded.

CLATTER! CRASH! BANG! CRASH! CRASH! CRASH!

160

"It's coming from the stairs!" shouted one of the guards.

"King Samuel knows that, you brainless fool!" Samuel yelled. "What *is* it?"

Whatever it was, it was making an almighty crashing noise, like horses riding through a field of metal. And it was coming closer and closer and getting louder and louder. Pirates began backing away from the stairs.

"No!" Samuel shouted. "Be ready for it! Stand firm!"

Glancing at each other nervously, the guards drew their weapons and pointed them at the stairs.

Diego and Carolina exchanged a puzzled look. If this was Jack coming to rescue them, he was being *really* unsubtle about it.

The noise came closer . . . and closer. . . .

161

CHAPTER THIRTEEN

Suddenly something charged around the corner of the stairs and burst into the throne room. It shot past them so quickly, the guards only had time to yell with surprise and fall over backwards. One of them fired his pistol into the ceiling, and a baboon shrieked angrily from the rafters.

"HIIII-YOOOOOOOO, Stripey!" bellowed the intruder—well, one of the intruders.

"It's Catastrophe Shane!" Carolina gasped.

"*What* is he *riding*?" asked Jean.

Catastrophe Shane, Jack's most incompetent crew member, was waving a pistol in the air with one hand and using the other to clutch the mane of the strangest horse Diego had ever seen. It was a bit smaller than a normal horse, and it was covered head-to-hoof in black-and-white stripes. It brayed loudly as it galloped around the throne room, bucking and jumping. It kicked two guards in the gut before the others got smart and hustled out of its way.

"I think it's a *zebra*," Carolina said, astonished. "I read about them, but I thought they were imaginary, like unicorns and hippos."

"Seize him!" King Samuel shouted, but the room was in chaos. Pirates fired their pistols into the air, which only made the zebra more enraged. It dashed wildly from side to side, nearly trampling guards as it went. Catastrophe Shane hung on for dear life, hollering with alarm.

"Heh-heh-heh." Carolina heard a familiar chuckle behind her, and then she felt the ropes around her wrists suddenly slacken and fall away. She whipped around and saw Grandmama slicing through Diego's bonds with a dagger.

"Never fails," said the old lady pirate. "The distraction trick. Samuel just fell for it twice in a row, didn't he? Hee-hee, this is the most fun I've had in centuries! Guess how many pirates I skewered on my way up here!"

"I don't want to know," Jean said quickly.

"And I was right about her, wasn't I?" Grandmama said, poking her dagger in Sarah's direction. Samuel's half-sister was standing on the throne, scowling down at the chaos with her hands on her hips. "Knew she looked too much like that hag Teresa. Must be her daughter. You should have let me drown her."

"Agreed," said Barbossa, snatching up his

sword as soon as he was free. "Now I'm going to teach her a lesson."

"Not if I get there first!" Grandmama crowed. She launched herself at the crowd of guards surging around the throne, and Barbossa chased after her.

Diego, Carolina, and Jean grabbed their swords, too, and began to fight their way over to Samuel and Jocard. Unfortunately, the Pirate Lord saw them coming and grabbed Jocard, using him as a shield, with his pistol digging into the small of Jocard's back.

"Don't come any closer!" he shouted. The three pirates from the *Pearl* clattered to a halt. "Stay back!"

"No, don't worry about me!" Jocard called, struggling. "Samuel must be stopped. Even if it means my death!"

"Well, that part can certainly be arranged," Samuel snarled, taking a step back. He glanced around at his pirates. Some of them were cowering behind the throne, hiding from the zebra. Others were doing battle with Grandmama and Barbossa, but from the wild, delighted look on Grandmama's face, it was pretty clear who was winning. And that wasn't counting the pirates who had already been knocked out and lay around the room, tripping up their fellow crew members as they fought.

"Look what you've done to my pirates. You'll pay for this," Samuel said, backing away toward the stairs. His strong arm was locked around Jocard's neck, dragging him along. Samuel paused at the top of the stairs, glaring at Diego, Carolina, and Jean.

"This isn't over," he growled. "I'll call my men back from the ships—and this time, there will be no second chances for you. I don't care how much I could have gotten for your sorry carcasses. You'll all die . . . except for this one. I'm taking this man with me."

"Oh, no you're not," a voice piped up behind him. An enormous bronze vase crashed into the back of Samuel's head.

The Pirate Lord's eyes went wide and then slowly drooped shut as he slumped to the floor. Jocard felt Samuel's arm slip free. He jumped away, grabbed Samuel's pistol where it had fallen, and turned to thank his rescuer.

"Marcella?" he said, astonished.

"*Marcella*?!" Diego, Carolina, and Jean cried in unison.

Jean's cousin stood at the top of the stairs. She tossed her hair and smiled triumphantly. "Who, me, saving the day? Why, yes, I am. Thank you for noticing." She lifted her chin and looked down her nose at Jocard. "Not that you deserved saving or anything. Stupid pirate captain, falling for a scheming wench like that." Marcella glared at Sarah, who was being sullenly escorted off the throne by Grandmama and Barbossa.

All around the room, Samuel's pirates were lying where they had fallen, either groaning in agony or unconscious. Catastrophe Shane had finally calmed down the zebra. The two of them were standing in a corner, and the zebra was munching placidly on the edge of a woven wall hanging.

"Got your traitor for you," Grandmama said to Jocard, shoving Sarah at him. The Portuguese woman scowled at all of them.

"I always knew she was evil," Marcella said. "Plus she has stupid hair."

"You'll be sorry for this when Samuel wakes up," Sarah said as Jean tied her hands tightly behind her.

"I have a feeling no one will be more sorry than Samuel when he wakes up," Jocard said. "You gave him quite a whack, Marcella."

Marcella preened. "If you want, I could do the same thing to her," she offered, nodding at Sarah.

"That won't be necessary," Jocard said, hiding a smile.

Suddenly they heard footsteps on the stairs. Someone else was running up to the throne room! Everyone drew their swords. There were still plenty of King Samuel's pirates around . . . and who knew how many were coming to fight them right now.

CHAPTER FOURTEEN

Jack skidded to a stop when he saw all the swords pointed at him.

"I say," he said, "that's not very friendly, is it?"

"Jack!" Carolina cried. "You're alive!"

"Oh, fabulous," Barbossa muttered.

"Don't sound so surprised," Jack said with a bow, flourishing his hat. "I'm remarkably hard to kill. Which is not an invitation to try," he added quickly.

Diego sheathed his sword and offered his

hand to help Jack jump over Samuel's prone body. Jack peered down at Samuel with an alarmed expression. "Had a bit too much rum, has he?" he said in a loud whisper to Diego.

"Actually, *I* defeated him," Marcella announced smugly.

"Blimey, and I thought she couldn't get any more insufferable," Jack said, rolling his eyes. "Hang on . . . why is that one all tied up?" He waved his hand at Sarah.

Diego told Jack the whole story as they tied up the rest of Samuel's pirates. But when Jack tried to tell his own story, nobody believed him.

"A hideous man-beast?" Jean said. "With black fur? Jack, are you sure *you* didn't have a bit too much rum?"

"Not in the least," Jack said, drawing himself up tall. "Well, only a jot. Barely a swig. My monstrous friend quite liked it, too, and I couldn't let him drink alone, could I? I think it might have been banana flavored." He hiccupped and looked thoughtful. "Yes, definitely banana flavored."

"A likely story," Barbossa sneered. "Battling monsters in the basement while we're up here doing all the hard work."

"See here!" Jack cried, looking injured. "If you don't believe me, just wait until you see old Benedict lying down there in the kitchens. He *still* hasn't woken up, can you believe it? I had to waste my fabulous dramatic exit line on an unconscious man. But I was running out of fruit, so it was really time to go before old beastie got restless again."

"You're sure it was Benedict Huntington?" Carolina asked. "Here? How did he knew we'd be here?"

Jack frowned. "That *is* a good question," he said, scratching his head. "Do you want to hear it?"

"Hear what?" said Diego.

"My dramatic exit line!" Jack cried. "Aren't you listening? Never fear, Huntington, for you will always look back and remember this remarkable day as that exact day when you *very nearly* captured the most famous of pirates, Jack Sparrow!"

He flung out his arms dramatically and paused as if waiting for applause. After a moment, when nothing happened, he dropped his arms and looked at his friends appraisingly.

"No?" he said. "Too much? Still needs work, doesn't it? I had a feeling it did."

Barbossa rolled his eyes and stomped off down the stairs to gather the rest of their crew.

Jack hopped over to Jocard, who was removing an old rusty-looking tobacco cutter from Samuel's belt. It looked worthless, but Jack knew it was Samuel's special piece of eight. It was what identified him as a Pirate Lord.

"It suits you, mate," Jack said, clapping Jocard on the back.

"Jack," Jocard said, standing up. "So glad you finally showed up to help."

"Well, I do what I can," Jack said modestly. "I guess this means you're Pirate Lord of the Atlantic Ocean now."

Jocard straightened his shoulders, and a broad smile slowly spread across his face. "I gather I am."

Jack waved his hands around. "So all this— this huge fort, all this treasure, all these lovely beasties—it's all yours."

Jocard shook his head. "No, that is not what I want. I just got my freedom, Jack Sparrow. I don't want to lose it again so soon by trapping myself inside cold stone walls. I want to be out on the seas on my ship, living like a true pirate. Speaking of which—men, signal the *Ranger*! We're taking the short route back to Libertalia!"

His pirates cheered heartily. No one wanted

to spend another night with the Madagascar rain-forest mosquitoes.

"Finally another Pirate Lord who sees things the way I do!" Jack said, shaking Jocard's hand with gusto. That was exactly how he felt about the freedom of the open seas and life aboard his ship. "So . . . incidentally . . . while we're liberating King Samuel of his gold sparklies . . ." He peered inquisitively down at the former Pirate Lord.

Jocard smiled. "I suppose this is what you're looking for?" He held up a vial of Shadow Gold on a leather strap. "It was around his neck."

"Well, it might be," Jack said casually, eyeing the Shadow Gold with a hungry expression.

"I'm not sure *you've* earned it," Jocard said, "but your pirates certainly have. So here you go." He tossed the vial to Jack.

"Well, that was delightfully easy," Jack said as he caught it.

"Easy!" Jean protested, waving his arms around at the wreckage of the throne room and the bumps and bruises on all the pirates.

"Well, it's all relative, mate," Jack said with a charming grin.

As his friend turned away, shaking his head in outrage, Jack slipped the vial into his coat pocket with trembling hands. He hadn't told anyone about the nightmares that had plagued him the night before. But once he drank this vial, he'd have at least a few days of blessed relief from the shadow-sickness, hopefully more. And then he only needed two more vials, and he'd be cured!

Don't drink the last vial, Jack. . . .

Jean's prophetic words rang in his head. What if they were true?

What if he drank the last vial . . . and someone else died for it?

CHAPTER FIFTEEN

Captain Teague was most satisfyingly astonished when the *Ranger* sailed back into Libertalia later that day carrying Jack, his crew, and Gentleman Jocard, the new Pirate Lord of the Atlantic Ocean. The only dark cloud over Jack's triumph was that when he'd returned to Samuel's kitchens, Benedict had vanished. Which not only meant that the Huntingtons were probably still out there looking for him, but also that he had no proof that he'd been having his own sword fight while everyone else was upstairs doing battle.

"All right," Teague said, tilting his bicorne hat back to look up at Jack, who was balancing along the rail of the *Ranger* while Jocard's pirates dropped anchor. "I'm a little impressed."

"They couldn't have done it without me," Grandmama smirked, popping up behind Jack and nearly startling him enough to send him toppling into the water. Luckily he windmilled his arms and caught his balance at the last moment.

"Or without me," Marcella added, wearing a matching pleased-with-herself expression.

Jack sighed. "Don't encourage them," he warned Teague.

Jocard came up to shake Jack's hand as the pirates began climbing off the *Ranger*. His new gold earrings shone in the sun.

"Carolina has been talking my ear off about

this Shadow Lord," Jocard said, patting the dark-haired girl on the shoulder. "It sounds like a great battle may be coming."

"That's what we hear," Jack said with a shrug.

"Well, my crew will be prepared to fight if necessary," said Jocard. Carolina beamed. "And now our debt is settled, Jack. I appreciate your help—such as it was—taking down King Samuel, but you have your Shadow Gold, and we are even."

"Fine by me," said Jack.

"So you understand," Jocard said with a smile, "that if I catch you in my waters again, I will have to blow you out of them."

"What?" Carolina cried.

"Of course!" Jack said, nodding as if this were obvious. He waved to Billy, who was trotting up the *Ranger*'s gangplank toward them.

"I am a Lord of the Brethren Court now," Jocard explained to Carolina. "And as the newest Pirate Lord, I have a reputation to establish. From what I hear, hobnobbing with Jack Sparrow isn't going to win me any friends."

Jack laughed. "Unfortunately, that is true." He tugged on his beard, looking sly. "But I have another proposition for you. Before you get all piratey on me, would you consider one more joint venture? One that would ensure pirates everywhere know the name of Gentleman Jocard?"

"Go on," Jocard said, looking intrigued.

"Oh, no," moaned Billy. "Jack, what are you dragging us into now?"

"Nothing terrible," Jack said blithely. "It's just that our next stop is Europe, savvy? We have two more vials to recover—one from Chevalle and one from the Pirate Lord of the Black Sea, whoever that is at the moment."

Carolina counted on her fingers. "You, Sao Feng, Mistress Ching, Villanueva, Sri Sumbhajee, and Gentleman Jocard, plus those two. Wait," she said, "that's only eight. Aren't there nine lords of the Brethren Court?"

"Oh, yes," Jack said, "but the last one is the Pirate Lord of the Caspian Sea. Ever heard of it?" Carolina started to nod, but he barreled on. "No, of course not, because it's an absolutely useless sea. I mean, it's completely landlocked. Really just a big lake. So whoever he is, he's not much of a pirate threat, eh? Sailing from one side to the other, going: 'I wonder where all the other pirates are!' Ha-ha!"

Jack and Jocard roared with laughter.

Nobody noticed Barbossa glowering furiously in the shadows.

"Anyway," Jack said, wiping away tears of laughter, "there's no chance *he* was counted strong enough to get a vial. No, I'm sure these guys have the last two. But it's going to be a lot harder to avoid the East India Trading

181

Company up there, now that they are looking for us. Not to mention the fact that the entire Spanish navy is probably out searching for a certain princess."

Carolina lowered her head.

"Plus it's *possible* the Shadow Lord will be there waiting for us," Jack said in a rush. "So—"

"Wait, *what*?" Billy demanded. "The Shadow Lord? How?"

"Well," Jack said, "he *may* have poked around in one of my nightmares. Just a bit. So he might know the Pirate Lords have the Shadow Gold. But he may not! He didn't seem like the brightest candle in the barrel, if you catch my drift."

"We're dead," Billy said, burying his head in his hands. "So, so, so, so, *so* dead."

"What I'm saying is a little extra firepower wouldn't go amiss," Jack finished with one of his charming grins.

"Sounds dangerous," Jocard said with a gleam in his eyes. "Why not? The whole Atlantic is mine now. All right, Jack Sparrow. The *Ranger* will accompany you to Europe."

"Oh, *no*," Marcella said loudly, elbowing her way into the conversation with Jean close behind her. "You mean we're stuck with your ugly mug? Please. You'll probably just abandon us out of nowhere without saying good-bye again, like a stupid pirate."

"Marcella, my savior," Jocard said gallantly. "How would you like to sail on the *Ranger* instead of the *Pearl* as we make our way north?"

Everyone goggled at him.

"You can't be serious," said Carolina.

"Best idea I've ever heard!" Jack burst out. "Take her! TAKE HER!"

"That's very kind of you," Jean said to Jocard, "but I'm afraid Marcella . . . well, she kind of hates you."

Marcella tossed her hair and stuck her nose in the air. "That's true," she said belligerently. "But—"

"But!" Jean cried, gaping at her.

"How's the food on this ghastly vessel?" Marcella asked, ignoring her cousin. "I mean, I never liked *you* . . . but I was okay with your jambalaya."

Jocard laughed. "Well, I must admit I don't cook it anymore," he said. "But I trained our cook myself, so . . . I'd say it's not too bad."

Marcella harrumphed. "I'm sure it's better than the nastiness they make us eat on his horrible ship," she said, shooting Jack a malevolent look. She tossed her hair again and flounced her skirts, and then finally she said, "Well, all right. But just for the food."

"I don't believe it," Jean sputtered.

"Quick! Make sail before she changes her mind!" Jack yelled, sprinting toward the gangplank.

"Are you sure about this?" Jean asked Jocard worriedly. "She's a little unusual. Sometimes she likes to shred things when she's really angry. But a glass of milk and some fish should calm her down . . . um . . . she really hates getting wet . . ."

"Don't fret," Jocard laughed, steering Jean off his ship. "I can handle Marcella."

"I don't need handling!" she shouted, flouncing around the deck. "And I haven't shredded anything in weeks! You're such a liar, Jean!"

"It'll be fun," Jocard reassured Jean. At the look on Jean's face, he amended, "Well, it won't be boring."

Carolina found Diego standing at the prow of the *Black Pearl*, staring off into the bay.

"Did you hear all that?" she asked, linking her arm through his.

"How could I not?" he said, smiling at her.

"Marcella's voice really . . . carries. I'm not sure I understand it, though. I didn't know she hated the food here *that* much."

Carolina started laughing. "It's not really about the food. You're such a boy." When he looked blank, she shoved his shoulder. "Marcella *likes* Jocard. That's why she's always complaining about him. And that's why she was so intent on tormenting Sarah."

"*Oh*," Diego said, comprehension dawning on his face. "Does that—does that mean she's forgotten about me?"

"Well, I'm not sure she *knows* how much she likes Jocard yet," Carolina said. "So you might not be off the hook . . . but the good news is, I'm not sure how much she really liked you in the first place."

Diego looked earnestly into her dark eyes. "Carolina," he said, "you must believe me. I have never had feelings for Marcella. I never

186

meant to kiss her. There is only one girl for me in the whole world and it's—"

"Oh, enough talking," Carolina said, and kissed him.

"Good-bye, Jackie," Teague said down on the dock, shaking Jack's hand.

"And good riddance," Grandmama added, stomping away with her cane.

"Come back again for the holidays," Teague suggested. "Auntie 'Quick Draw' McFleming will be visiting with all your little cousins."

Jack shuddered. "I'd rather be eaten by turtles," he admitted.

"I'm here if you ever need your hide saved again!" Grandmama shouted from the end of the dock. "I love a nice, gory battle! Anytime!"

"How old *is* she?" Jack asked, trying to do the math in his head.

"Safer not to ask," said Teague. "Now Jackie,

you will take care of yourself, won't you? Don't be a hero. Be a pirate. If there's a Shadow Lord after you, do what a pirate would, you hear?"

"You mean survive?" Jack said. "Yeah, I'm pretty good at that."

"Not just surviving," Teague said with a dark expression. "Make sure that whatever you choose . . . you can still live with yourself at the end."

Jack watched Teague stroll back to the streets of Libertalia. He thought again of Jean's ominous visions of the future. Jack didn't like hard choices. Better not to think about it until he had to.

Up on the deck of the *Ranger*, Marcella was leaning against the rail and staring into her mirror, admiring the way the wind blew through her hair. She glanced around to make sure the pirates were busy at the other end of the ship, and then she grimaced into the mirror to check that there was nothing in her teeth.

"This will be much nicer," she said conversationally to the mirror, running her fingers through her hair. "The *Ranger* is *so* much cleaner than the *Pearl*. I won't have to share hammock space with Carolina. And I won't have to listen to Jack capering around being a lunatic all day long."

Marcella heard a strange noise, almost like a muffled shriek of rage, come from the mirror. She shook her head, wiggled her finger in her ear, and then peered closer at the glassy surface.

All of a sudden, a face appeared in the mirror—and it wasn't Marcella's!

She came very close to screaming and throwing the mirror overboard. But then she recognized the face.

"Barbara!" she cried with delight. It was her elegant friend, the one that Marcella had helped stow away on the *Pearl* on the voyage from Hong Kong to India. The last time Marcella had seen her, right before the battle at Suvarnadurg, Barbara had given her the mirror as a memento of their friendship (or so Marcella thought).

"Marcella!" Barbara said in a sugary sweet voice. "I've missed you so much!"

"This is crazy." Marcella gasped. She turned the mirror over and checked the other side. "How are you doing this?" She shook the mirror as if she expected Barbara to come tumbling out. The well-dressed redhead looked queasy when Marcella peered into the mirror again. "Is it magic?" Marcella bubbled on. "I didn't know there was anything like this in the world!" She poked at Barbara's face with her fingers.

"Stop that!" Barbara snapped. "Marcella, my patience is wearing thin. Did I just hear you say you're leaving the *Pearl*?"

"I am!" Marcella said. "Isn't it terrific? I'm

going to sail on the *Ranger* instead. It's *so* much nicer, you wouldn't believe." She paused, blinking, as she registered what Barbara had said. "Hey, wait a second. You were listening to me?"

"You *cannot* leave the *Pearl*!" Barbara shouted. "You must stay with Jack Sparrow!"

"But we are staying with Jack!" Marcella protested. "We're all going to France together."

"France," Barbara said icily. She turned and glanced over her shoulder. "Write that down."

"I think I can remember bloody *France*," said a male voice in the background.

"Who's that?" Marcella asked, squinting. "Are you with someone? Is that a ship you're on?"

As Barbara turned back to Marcella, she jostled the mirror on her end. For a moment, the room behind her spun, and Marcella caught a glimpse of the man standing beside Barbara. She gasped.

"That's Benedict Huntington!" Marcella cried. "Diego warned me about him! He's the one that's been chasing us! He's totally evil!"

"On the contrary," Benedict said, leaning over to stare coolly into Marcella's eyes. "I serve the Company, whatever they need me to do."

"You were working together this whole time," Marcella realized, her eyes starting to fill with tears. Everything Barbara had told her—all their whispered conversations on the trip to India— all of it was fake! "Barbara, you *lied* to me. You said you were my *friend*."

"Oh, spare me the histrionics," Barbara said, rolling her eyes. "Listen, Marcella, we can be very good friends to you. Keep telling us where Jack is and what he's planning, and we can save you from this revolting pirate life you hate so much. If you help us catch him, we can guarantee your safety, and probably a big reward as well. Just think of all the pretty dresses and fans and gloves you'll be able to buy! Just like mine! And you'll never have to set foot on a ship again. You'll be able to live wherever you want to. Maybe France? I think you'd quite like it there."

"A life of ease and luxury," Benedict said smarmily. "All in exchange for a little information. What could be easier than that?"

Marcella bit her lip. "But . . . what about Jean? Will he be safe, too?"

Benedict's eyes turned cold. "There will be no leniency for the other pirates," he snapped.

"They're all wanted men," Barbara agreed. "You understand, Marcella. This deal is for you alone."

"I will see every pirate punished," Benedict growled. "Especially the Pirate Lords of the Brethren Court. And most especially *Jack Sparrow*."

Marcella was sorely tempted. She'd never really been rich, but she could imagine how wonderful it would be. Having everything she wanted . . . being treated like a real lady . . . going to balls and living in a big house . . .

She looked away from the mirror, thinking, and saw Jocard strolling among his men, giving quiet orders and making suggestions as they prepared the ship to sail. He saw her watching him and waved with an amused smile.

"Marcella?" Barbara demanded. "Marcella, don't be a fool. This is your only chance. Get back to the *Pearl* right now, and everything will be just fine."

Marcella took a deep breath, snapped the mirror shut, and tossed it overboard. It landed with a tiny splash in the harbor. She could see its silvery shape shimmering like an exotic fish as it slowly sank through the clear, blue-green water.

She still hated pirates. She wouldn't mind getting rid of a few in particular; it would be lovely to see Jack and Carolina swing from the end of a rope. But she couldn't betray them all the way the Huntingtons wanted her to—especially not Jean—or Jocard, who had promised her jambalaya for dinner that night.

On the other hand, she also didn't want to get into trouble. She decided not to tell anyone about the magical spying mirror. It would be terrible if they blamed her for how Benedict always seemed to find them. And it wasn't *really* her fault. After all, she hadn't *known* it was a supernatural mirror!

As the *Ranger* slowly pulled out of the bay, its white sails billowing like morning clouds, Marcella watched the horizon uneasily.

Benedict and Barbara knew about France now. They had contacts in Europe who would be more than happy to lay their hands on a pair of Pirate Lords.

And Marcella was the only one who knew that the pirates might be sailing right into a trap.

EPILOGUE

A full moon floated over the city of Marseilles, France. Its silvery light was reflected in the soft ripples of the sea around the port. Even in the dark of night, several of the ships lining the dock were bustling with activity as men loaded and unloaded cargo.

Two sailors staggered along one of the docks, joking about the beautiful French women they were hoping to meet while their ship was in port.

One of them squinted out at the sea.

"Hey, François," he said. "Am I drunker than I thought? Is that a ship coming in?"

François tilted his head, looking puzzled. "But—there is no wind."

"And the oars aren't moving," said his friend.

They stared at the ship as it glided closer and closer in eerie silence. The sails were slack and still. There was no movement on the deck. It looked almost as if it were made of dark clouds and shadows barely visible in the moonlight.

"Is it the *Flying Dutchman*?" François whispered, his voice trembling with terror.

Louis's eyes went to the black flag hanging limp at the top of the main mast. "No. That's a Jolly Roger," he said, taking a step back. "But whose?"

The sailors watched as the flag stirred slightly. They could barely make out a white skeleton . . . and a red heart.

"Villanueva," François breathed. "But where is his crew? Where is he?"

"I don't know," Louis answered. "But I'm not staying to find out!" He took off down the nearest alleyway, tripping over his feet as he ran. François paused only a moment, staring at the mysterious vessel, before turning and running after his friend.

Other sailors along the dock fell silent and stopped what they were doing when they saw the ship approaching. There were no hails, no one waving from the deck, no sign of life at all. The ship sailed mercilessly forward at the same steady pace. It was aiming for an open berth along the dock.

With barely a whisper of sound on the water, the *Centurion* pulled up to the dock and then it just . . . stopped. No one saw the anchor drop. No ropes were thrown from the deck to tie the ship in place. It just stopped.

Suddenly a man appeared on the deck. He strode slowly to the rail. Stories differ about what happened next, but more than one sailor claimed that he saw the gangplank slide out and lower itself to the dock *all by itself* . . . with no human help at all.

The man stepped down the gangplank, twisting a ring on his finger. He was short and round, with a large feathered hat, but he was definitely *not* Villanueva. It was hard to see his face clearly. It almost seemed as if dark shadows were wrapped around his neck like a scarf. Several sailors said they thought they saw black cats twining around his legs as he walked—but then the cats vanished into thin air, like smoke.

Clop . . . clop . . . clop . . .

The man's boots echoed on the wooden dock as he walked toward the city, gazing menacingly around him.

What the sailors could not see was the scene inside the *Centurion*.

They could not see the crew bound and gagged and lying miserably in the brig.

They could not see the proud Pirate Lord, Villanueva himself, tied firmly to a chair in his cabin. With a muffled, angry grunt, Villanueva tried to struggle free from his bonds, then froze as his captors poked him sharply in the ribs.

His eyes traveled slowly up the hideous creatures standing guard over him. The closest one frightened him most of all. It looked like a strange construction of his own swabbing mop, his spyglass, a long red curtain, and a wicked-looking dagger. But it was alive—it was moving! Shadows wreathed around the ordinary objects, making them look like demons from his worst nightmares. The sailor really felt as if his spyglass were glaring at him.

Villanueva shivered and bowed his head.

Who could have known? Who would have suspected Henry, the lazy, fat pirate that Villanueva had "stolen" from Jack in Tortuga? Who would ever have guessed that he was the Shadow Lord himself?

Perhaps Jack knew. That would be just like him, to trick Villanueva into taking the most dangerous pirate in the world onto his ship.

A growl rumbled deep in Villanueva's throat. He only hoped he lived long enough to see the Shadow Lord kill Jack Sparrow.

Out on the dock, a sailor was shaking with fear as the Shadow Lord stopped beside him. Piercing black eyes seemed to stare at him from a pit of shadow.

"Tell me," hissed the Shadow Lord in French, "where I can find the Pirate Lord Chevalle."

"We don't know anything about Chevalle," the sailor squeaked. "Piracy is of course forbidden, and we wouldn't have anything to do with—"

A thick band of dark clouds shot out of the Shadow Lord's ring and wrapped itself around the sailor's throat.

"Tell me," the Shadow Lord repeated.

Clawing at his throat, the sailor managed to gasp out directions.

"*Merci beaucoup*," said the Shadow Lord. He dropped the sailor in a quivering heap on the dock.

Pulling on his gloves, the Shadow Lord set off into Marseilles with vengeance and murder glittering in his eyes.

Don't miss the next thrilling volume of

DISNEY
PIRATES of the CARIBBEAN

LEGENDS OF THE
BRETHREN COURT

Day of the Shadow

This is it! The stunning conclusion to the swashbuckling Brethren Court series. Be here when Jack finally encounters the Shadow Lord, while the fate of his crew—and the world— hang in the balance!